FLIGHT OF THE HERON

On her deathbed, Christie's mother confides to her daughter that she has family she never knew existed — grandparents, a great-aunt, and an uncle — and elicits a promise from Christie to travel to Devon to meet them. When she arrives, she's surprised to find another man living there: the leonine and captivating Lucas Grant. But when her grandmother decides to change her will and leave Christie a sizeable inheritance, it's soon all too evident that someone wants to get rid of her, and both her uncle and Lucas have a motive . . .

SUSAN UDY

◆

FLIGHT
OF THE
HERON

Complete and Unabridged

LINFORD
Leicester

First published in Great Britain in 2015

First Linford Edition
published 2015

A catalogue record for this book is available
from the British Library.

ISBN 978–1–4448–2481–0

Published by
F. A. Thorpe (Publishing)
Anstey, Leicestershire

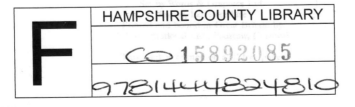

1

Christie Wakeham stared at the man who had just walked through the door. He couldn't be a member of the family — could he? He bore absolutely no resemblance to the other people in the room: her grandparents; her great-aunt, and her uncle. He was also many years younger than any of them, and tall — six feet one or two, she guessed — with a build that suggested regular and strenuous work-outs.

But the most noticeable thing about him was his strangely leonine quality, made all the more striking by the colour of his hair — a rich, tawny gold. His eyes were the colour of toffee, flecked with amber glints, and they were fixed unwaveringly upon her. His nose, she saw, when her gaze dragged itself away from his, was ever so slightly aquiline; a marked contrast to his mouth with its

1

full bottom lip. And as for his jawline, that looked as if it had been chiselled from a solid block of granite.

All of that, taken with the somewhat grim expressions now decorating three of the other four faces — her grandfather seemed the only one pleased to see her — had her wishing to heaven that she'd obeyed her initial instinct and had stayed well away from Heron House. Even the dog — a Doberman, she thought — was growling throatily and menacingly at her from its position at the feet of the man she presumed was her uncle, a man whose florid complexion and portly build strongly suggested he'd regularly and lavishly partaken of the good things in life: namely, food and alcohol. He was the complete antithesis of her grandfather, who was markedly slender, so much so that the bones of his face were clearly etched beneath his milky, age-spotted skin.

It was at that point that she wondered whether she should simply get to her feet and walk out, because it was more than evident that she wasn't welcome.

Whatever had possessed her to turn up unannounced and unexpected? But then again, what real choice had she had? And why hadn't her mother warned her about the sort of reception she might encounter? Or, with the passing of the years, had she forgotten how bleak and hostile this place and its inhabitants were? She must have, otherwise why would she have wanted Christie to come, thereby placing herself at the mercy of these hard-faced people? After all, it had been Laura herself, who had run away from it all those years ago. That in itself spoke volumes.

Her thoughts reverted to the day — when was it, nine, ten weeks ago? — that Christie had gazed down in anguish at the woman lying in the bed. She hadn't needed to be told that her mother, Laura, was dying. The evidence was there, plain to see: the emaciated body, the grey skin, the sunken eyes and cheeks, the bloodless lips, the lank hair — they had all told the same stark tale. The end was near.

'Christie,' Laura had weakly whispered. Christie had leant down, placing her ear practically against her mother's mouth, the better to hear what she wanted to say. 'I need to tell you something. Something I should have told you long ago.' She drew a rasping breath, as if, by some miracle that would imbue her with the strength to go on. It didn't. Her voice quivered. 'You have more family: grandparents, a great-aunt, an uncle . . . '

'What?' Christie jerked upright and stared at her mother. She couldn't believe what she was hearing. Was it for real, or was it a fantasy brought about by the tumour that was systematically and ruthlessly destroying her mother's brain? But Laura sounded lucid; a rarity of late. And if what she was saying was true, that Christie had other family, then why had her parents always led her to believe that there was no one else; that it was just the three of them?

'I'm sorry. I should have told you long ago. Adam wasn't my first husband. Another man was: his older brother, Rafe. We were together for three years. I-I left Rafe for Adam. We ran away.'

Christie couldn't speak, so shocked was she by what her mother was telling her.

'Rafe was . . . ' Laura was struggling to simply draw breath by this time. Christie bent low again, the better to hear the faltering words. ' . . . a difficult man to live with. We were very unhappy together. Adam — Adam was always there. We fell in love.' She smiled weakly; tenderly. 'We couldn't remain at the house.'

'What house? Where?'

'Heron House, in Wellford. Devon. Adam and Rafe's parents' house. We all lived there — together — for a while. Adam and I left. Rafe divorced me and Adam and I married.'

'I was . . . am I . . . Adam's daughter?' Oh God, supposing the father she'd adored hadn't been her biological father? Supposing it had been this Rafe? A deep-seated dread engulfed her. Was the world in which she'd always felt so secure about to change — forever?

'Oh yes.'

'So why didn't you tell me any of this before?' Christie's voice rose. She couldn't help it. The knowledge that the people she'd trusted so implicitly, loved so deeply, had kept something so vital from her, so important, induced an emotion that came dangerously close to hysteria. Her thoughts whirled frantically as she struggled to take it all in. She had a family, a whole other family, about whom she knew nothing, living in a place she'd never heard of.

'Your father didn't want to. He was afraid that when you were old enough you'd contact them.' Laura was fighting even harder for breath, for the strength to go on, but Christie could see she was

6

weakening, fast.

'Mum, have a rest,' she urged, her emotions instantly calming in the face of her mother's struggle to breathe. Laura must have had her reasons for such a huge deception. Her mother was — always had been — the most genuine, honest person. Christie would have trusted her with her life; she did trust her with her life.

'No. I have to tell you — now. There's not much time. Your father was afraid his mother would interfere in your upbringing; take over.'

Christie put out a hand and grasped Laura's, trying to lend her some of her own strength.

'He didn't want that. She could be very domineering.'

'So why are you telling me now?' Christie felt as sick as her mother looked.

'I want you to go to them when I've gone.' Laura's voice had sunk so low that Christie had to strain to hear her words.

'You're not going anywhere,' she cried.

Laura's eyes closed wearily. 'Let's not kid ourselves, darling. We both know I'm dying.'

'No.' Christie's voice broke as tears filled her eyes. She couldn't lose her mother; she had no one else. This family — she'd never heard of them, didn't know them. They weren't her real family; a real family was one you grew up amongst. It meant a grandmother who loved you, spoiled you; a grandfather who doted upon you; an uncle who —

She dashed the tears away, not wanting her mother to see her distress. These people were strangers to her; she would be a stranger to them. They might not want to know her — what then? After all, she was the daughter of the two people who'd deserted them. Did they even know that their youngest son, Adam, had died two and a half years ago? And yet, she had no one else. Her mother had been an only child whose own parents had died many years before, which meant Christie had no memory of them.

'Yes. And I don't want you to be alone. Promise me you will go to them. Promise . . . ' Laura's thin fingers, surprisingly strong all of a sudden, tightened their grip on Christie's.

'I promise.' The words were wrung from Christie. The last thing she wanted to do was go and find an unknown family.

'There's a box in the cupboard in the sitting room. The key — the key to it is in my dressing table — top drawer. Open the box. There are letters . . . ' Laura paused; what little strength she had left was rapidly fading. 'Read them. Forgive me, darling. I love you. I'll always be with you, never forget that.'

The blue-veined eyelids closed and they were the last lucid words that Laura Wakeham spoke. Moments afterwards, she lapsed into a coma, dying three days later.

* * *

A couple of weeks passed before Christie felt sufficiently strong to go in search of the box and the key that her mother had spoken of. The box was made of oak, constructed in the style of a miniature trunk, with a domed lid and ornate brass corners. She'd never seen it before, so her mother must have placed it there only recently.

Once she knew she was dying?

Christie unlocked it and, just as her mother had said, found three letters. They were the only things inside. She lifted them out and found the earliest one. She pulled the single sheet of paper out of the unsealed envelope and began to read. It must have been written right after Adam and Laura left, while the anger and hurt were still fresh.

There were no preliminaries of any sort. It bluntly asked:

How could you do it, Adam? How? Rafe is destroyed. Whatever possessed you to make you behave in such a manner? To make you so cruel? I will never forgive you, you or Laura. Nor will your father. We feel such disappointment in you. That a son of ours could behave in such a way. From now on, your father and I have only one son, Rafe. You have forfeited any inheritance, I trust you realize that.

Venetia Wakeham

The next one was dated just four years ago.

Adam, it began, I hope this letter will reach you. I know it's been a long time since I last wrote but I have decided to let bygones be bygones and put the troubles behind us. Your father desperately misses you — as do I. Please, won't you come home? You can bring Laura. I'm sure, if we try, we can all learn to forgive and forget — even Rafe. Don't let me down.

Your mother, Venetia Wakeham

She regarded the last letter for a long time before reading it.

Laura, it said — it was dated two years and four months ago — *thank you for letting us know of Adam's death. I deeply regret all that happened, especially the fact that Adam didn't feel he could respond to my request for you both to return to Heron House. Now, of course, it's too late. Victor is beside himself with grief. So many years wasted . . .*

There was no mention of Christie. Just as she'd known nothing of them, they evidently knew nothing of her. Adam had clearly not responded to any of the letters. The break between him and his family had been total. Yet, they obviously knew where Adam and Laura were, otherwise her grandmother couldn't have written, so one of her parents must have relented and had some sort of contact, at some time. Her mother? With her soft heart and boundless capacity for forgiveness, it would seem the most likely.

It was a full month after that before Christie could bring herself to do a Google search and locate Wellford. It was situated close to Dartmoor. A world away, it seemed to Christie. And not just in miles. Her heart lurched at the mere thought of the prospect ahead of her. She really didn't want to do this.

So it didn't help that her current boyfriend, Toby, had no scruples about echoing Christie's misgivings.

'You know nothing about these people. Do you even know whether they're still alive? That they're still there, at this place — Heron House?'

'Well, the last letter was dated just over two years ago.'

'A hell of a lot could have happened in two and a bit years, especially to people their age.'

'Well, I would have thought they were still there. I mean,' she said, frowning, 'wouldn't someone have written if anything like that had happened?'

But would they have if Adam had ignored their letters?

'Lord knows! I can't believe it — a secret family.'

'I know, I can barely believe it myself.' Maybe Toby was right — she shouldn't go.

'Look, if you're really set on going, I'll come with you.'

'No, Toby. If I decide to go, it's something I have to do myself — alone. Someone else's presence could make things even more awkward than I suspect they'll already be. I'm sure they'll be just as shocked to learn about me as I've been to learn about them.'

Toby eyed her, doubt clouding his eyes. 'But supposing you get there and then want to stay?'

Ah, so that's what he was worried about. She tried to reassure him.

'I can't stay; I have the house to sell. Anyway, all my plans for the future are centred here.'

'I know, but once you're there who knows how you'll feel?'

Christie shrugged. 'How can I say for certain? As you've already pointed out, I know nothing about them.'

'Exactly,' Toby exploded. 'Christie, I

14

love you. I don't want to lose you.'

Christie was startled. A declaration of love was the very last thing she'd expected; wanted, even. She wasn't ready for it. She had plans — as she'd just said — and she wasn't at all sure that they included Toby; at least, not on a long-term basis.

She'd been going out with him now for about six months, give or take. She liked him and he was fun to be with. His sense of humour, his dry wit, had entertained her throughout many an evening that without him would have been deadly dull. But love? She hadn't even considered that, and Toby, till this moment, hadn't given as much as a hint that that was the way he felt. There had been kisses, naturally; they were normal, red-blooded people. But those, too, had been kept light, nothing too heavy. She'd genuinely believed that that was what they had both wanted.

She stared at him. 'I don't know what to say, Tobes. Are you sure?'

'Of course I'm sure. It's not something I'd say lightly. The truth is . . . '

He hesitated then. 'I've never said it to anyone before.'

'Oh, Toby, I just don't know whether I feel the same way.'

'No, I know, which is why I've said nothing before. But maybe, given time, you might.'

'Well,' she murmured, 'I s'pose.'

'Christie — ' He grabbed hold of her by the shoulders, his tone one of urgency now. ' — please, don't go. I'll miss you, and I'm so afraid you won't come back, house to sell or not.' He pulled her in then, closing the gap between their lips, his kiss unlike any that he given her before. It was full of frustration and unrequited passion. It was as if he were determined to make her feel the way he did.

And she did feel something; a piercing stab of emotion. She just wasn't sure whether it was love or not. Maybe, as he'd said, given time she would find it in her to return his feelings? Her heart did lift when she saw him, just not in the rapturous way she would have expected if she loved him. And she enjoyed being with him. So — was that love? And how would she know if it was? She'd never believed herself to be in love before. How did you even recognize it?

Toby deepened the kiss, forcing her lips apart, forcing a response. His arms tightened around her before all of a sudden he let go. 'See — you do feel something. You wouldn't be able to kiss me like that if you didn't.'

She stared at him. Could he possibly be right?

'Give it — give us — time, please,' he begged. 'Don't leave now.' He reached for her again. This time she deftly evaded his grasp.

'Toby, I have to go. I promised. But I'll be back. I will,' she vowed, in the face of his obvious scepticism. 'And then we'll see how things are between us.'

'Promise me.'

Christie sighed. Promises. She was beginning to feel weighed down by them. 'Yes, okay. I promise.'

'And you'll ring me if you're at all unsure of anything, anything at all. Promise?'

Oh lord, another promise. She nodded.

'Okay, I'll keep you to it all.' And at last he grinned at her, satisfied for now with what she'd said and done.

Even so, it was a further month before Christie felt ready to pack a bag and embark upon the drive to Wellford, where she had booked a room in the only hotel that the village boasted. Although her grief had lessened fractionally, a deep sense of loss, as well as an unutterable loneliness, had stayed with her; so much so that it took only a fleeting memory to cause the tears to well. Despite that, though, she was more in control of her emotions, fortunately. The last thing she had wanted was to arrive weeping on her grandparents' doorstep. What sort of first impression would that make?

She didn't reach the village until late

afternoon, having got lost in the last few miles of tortuously winding high-hedged lanes, after which she decided to wait until the following day to present herself at Heron House, when she hoped she would feel more in control of herself and at least partly prepared for what she suspected would prove to be an ordeal. Her existence and arrival were going to come as an enormous shock to them. As great a shock as learning of their existence had been to her. She hadn't written to them, not knowing what to say. How could she announce by letter that they had a granddaughter? It was something that needed to be done face-to-face.

Doubt swamped her, just as it had whenever she'd considered what it was she had to do; what she'd so reluctantly promised to do. However, do it she must, she'd finally decided. It had been the last thing her mother had asked of her. She couldn't let her down. So, the next morning she duly presented herself at the hotel's reception desk and asked the girl standing there for directions to the house.

The girl's response wasn't an encouraging one. She sniffed and said, 'Not many people go there, so I've heard.' She stared at Christie, her expression all of a sudden one of unmistakable curiosity. 'They don't encourage visitors.' In the face of Christie's total silence, she went on, 'Well, anyway, you go out of the village and turn left at the first crossroads. The house is about three miles along that road. On the right.' Again, her gaze was full of curiosity. 'Know the Wakehams, do you?'

'No.' The girl clearly didn't realize that Christie's surname was Wakeham and Christie didn't enlighten her. She hadn't been on the desk when Christie arrived; another girl had been. She hadn't reacted at all to Christie's name, so maybe she was a newcomer to the village, drafted in for the summer season.

'Hmm, I see. Well, good luck then.'

Good luck? Was she going to need it? Her heart sank. Maybe Toby had been right and she should just turn round and go home? No one need ever know she'd been here — apart from herself, of course. And therein lay her problem. She simply couldn't bring herself to renege on that final promise to her mother, no matter how apprehensive she was of whatever lay ahead of her.

She duly followed the receptionist's directions to Heron House, where the first obstacle she found herself confronted with was a pair of wrought-iron gates. They were closed and at least ten feet high, a very effective means of barring anyone's way in. That would have been impediment enough, but then she noticed the long row of iron palings that flanked them on either side. They were virtually the same height as the gates, with lethally pointed tops, and ran alongside the road for a considerable distance in both directions before disappearing into dense hedgerows of holly and prickly hawthorn. There was no pretence of welcoming unheralded visitors. Indeed, the whole set up smacked of a determination to be left alone. Well, maybe she should heed the warning signs and turn around and leave?

She didn't. Instead, she climbed from the car and stood, peering through the gates at the driveway. It twisted and turned between a tangle of high shrubs and towering trees, dark and full of gloom and, despite the brightness of the day, menacing. So when the sun dived behind a large cloud, the journey along its shadowy length presented an even more intimidating prospect. A pair of rooks flapped noisily overhead, their calls harsh, startling her. She glanced upwards. Their blackness against the sky looked . . . well, sinister. Images of all the horror films she'd watched over the years flashed into her head. There were invariably black birds flying around. They seemed to define the human fear of darkness, malevolence, devilish practices. Christie shook herself free of the heebie-jeebies that such thoughts induced and returned her gaze to the driveway ahead of her. There was no sign of a house — of any sort of human habitation, in fact.

Oh for heaven's sake, get it over with, she told herself. Nothing could be as bad as imagined terrors — at least, she hoped not. With hands that shook, she pushed at one of the gates. She didn't know whether to be relieved or dismayed when it gave immediately beneath her touch. They weren't even latched, she saw. It was then that she noticed the twin circular plaques centrally placed on each gate; they were individually etched with the head of a grey heron, turned to face each other.

She gulped. Something had just occurred to her. Supposing there were guard dogs? It looked that sort of place. Maybe she should have phoned ahead after all, simply to ensure there was someone waiting to greet her; to fend the dogs off. Again, she chided herself. She was being downright ridiculous now. And face it, given the circumstances under which her parents had left, they might well have refused to see her if she'd given them warning of her imminent arrival. And that meant she wouldn't have been able to keep her promise to her mother. At least this way, and even if they turned her away, she would have done what she'd said she'd do, and in so doing could put it behind her and get on with the rest of her life — alone, if that was what Fate had decreed for her.

Tears stung her eyes at the thought. She dashed them away. She refused to turn up at her grandparents' door red-eyed and weeping.

More firmly now, she opened the other gate and then returned to her car and gingerly made her way along the shadowy driveway. She turned a corner and there, looming before her, was the house. She practically stood on the brakes. My God! It was like something out of a Grimm's fairy-tale. Or a nightmare, her mind unhelpfully suggested.

Huge, built of grey stone, with corner turrets and steeply sloping silver-grey roofs above row upon row of mullioned windows, their glass panes glistening in the sunlight that had burst through once more, it was a true Gothic monstrosity. A modern-day Dracula could easily be waiting for her inside, fangs at the ready.

Although she knew that yet again she was being stupidly fanciful, her already wavering courage completely deserted her and, literally quivering with nerves, she crept forward to park in front of the main entrance, a rather forbidding-looking iron-studded oak door.

What sort of people would live in a house like this? was the question that hammered at her. She snorted. She was beginning to sound like the chap who'd hosted that program she'd loved as a young girl — what was it? *Through the Keyhole?* Yes, that was it. Her memories, as fond as they were, completely failed to assuage her apprehension, however. The house still looked as if its rightful place would be in the wilds of Transylvania!

The driveway had broadened out here into a huge sweep of gravel upon which three cars were standing, one of which was a rather ancient but still-grand Bentley. Her grandparents' car? The other two were modern: a gleaming white Mercedes convertible and a large dark grey BMW.

She climbed from her own more modest Fiesta and just stood there, gazing at this formidable building. A harsh 'kraak, kraak' had her looking up, wondering what she was going to find herself looking at now. It was a heron, its stick-like legs protruding horizontally from beneath its silver-grey body as it glided majestically over her.

She smiled then, albeit shakily. Could its appearance be a good omen? That both she and the house's namesake should arrive at the same time? She desperately wanted it to be. Which was quite something for someone who professed to be not the least bit superstitious. A judgement that, taking into account the disproportionate agonies and anxieties of the past few moments over everything that she had experienced, she was starting to revise. Still, feeling marginally more cheerful in the wake of this sighting — mercifully, the rooks had disappeared, too — she rang the doorbell.

A plump, rosy-cheeked woman answered her ring. She looked far too young to be Christie's grandmother; she couldn't be more than forty-five or thereabouts.

'Yes?' The single word was distinctly unwelcoming. Which wasn't entirely unexpected, taking into account the hotel receptionist's words.

'I wonder, could I speak to Mrs Wakeham? Venetia Wakeham?'

After her initial coolness, the woman peered closely at Christie and asked, 'Is she expecting you?'

'No.'

'Only she doesn't usually see anyone who isn't expected, although you could well prove the exception to that,' she murmured in conclusion. 'What name shall I tell Mrs Wakeham?'

Christie took a deep breath. This was it: crunch time. She'd either be welcomed in, or summarily thrown out.

'Christie Wakeham.'

'Ah.'

'Who is it, Delia?' a voice called from somewhere inside the house. 'Don't just stand there with the door open. There's a chill breeze even though it's late June.'

There was the sound of footsteps on a stone flagged floor before the door was dragged wider and a much older woman appeared. Her gaze impaled Christie right where she stood.

'It's a young lady calling herself Christie Wakeham, Mrs Wakeham.'

An expectant smile belatedly decorated Delia's face. Christie didn't need to ask why. As she stared at the old woman, it was as if she were looking into her own future. This, then, was her grandmother. They were too much alike for her not to be. There, on a level with her own, were the same violet-coloured eyes, faded slightly with age it was true; the same heart-shaped face with its neat nose and sculptured cheekbones, albeit the skin was wrinkled. They even had the same shaped mouth, though Christie's fuller, of course. The only thing that was vastly different was the hair. Where Christie's shoulder-length bob ranged from streaks of dark caramel to creamy honey, Venetia's loosely wound bun was iron-grey. But Christie wouldn't mind betting that once it had been of a similar colour. Even their build was the same: slender, but with curves in all the right places. Although the older woman was now heavier than Christie, Christie guessed that once upon a time her grandmother had enjoyed the same vital statistics as she possessed: thirty-seven, twenty-four, thirty-six.

The violet eyes glittered, their stare penetrating and highly critical. Here was a woman who wouldn't suffer fools or pretenders gladly. Christie's heart missed a beat — well, several, in fact — and her breath caught in her throat.

'Christie Wakeham? I don't know of anyone in the family of that name. What kind of fool name is that anyway? Christie, indeed!'

Christie bit back her instinctive and

angry response. She didn't want to upset her grandmother, not at this early stage. She wanted, at least, to try and get along with her. It was, after all, her dying mother's wish that she do so. 'I'm your granddaughter, Adam and Laura's daughter.'

Venetia's face visibly paled and she swayed slightly. Delia swiftly placed a hand beneath her elbow. The old woman shook her off. 'I'm perfectly all right, Delia. Don't fuss. It will take more than something like this to upset me.' Nonetheless, she continued to stare long and hard at Christie before finally saying, 'Humph, you'd better come in then and explain yourself.' She promptly turned to walk stiff-backed into the house. She exuded dignity and self-possession.

Christie, for all her indignation over her grandmother's reaction to her name, felt the first glimmerings of admiration for the old lady. Apart from that initial paling she had barely shown any emotion at all, and that must have taken a will of iron. Christie glanced at Delia as she passed through the doorway and, to her surprise, saw the woman's one eyelid lower in a wink. Christie smiled in open relief. If that wink was sincere, she had one friend, at least, here.

'And you are?' she asked Delia now.

'Delia Gillespie — housekeeper, cook, and general dogsbody,' she concluded in a whisper. 'Matt, my husband, is the gardener-cum-chauffeur when needed.'

'Well, are you coming in?' Venetia's brusque tones interrupted them before Christie could glean any more information from the woman.

Venetia led her into what was clearly a library, from the sight of the packed bookshelves that towered from the floor to the ceiling, although one wall was practically filled with windows and a cavernous fireplace took pride of place in another. There was even a set of rather grand library steps to enable one to reach the top shelves.

'Sit over there, facing the window. I want to have a good look at you,' Venetia autocratically instructed.

She'd never been ordered about in such a fashion before; both her parents had been gentle people who wouldn't have dreamt of issuing commands in the way that this old woman was doing. But despite her aversion to her grandmother's authoritative manner, Christie meekly went and sat in the straight-backed armchair which her grandmother had indicated. Venetia seated herself in the one opposite. It meant that with her back to the windows, Venetia's face was in shadow, whereas Christie sat blinking in the sunlight, barely able to see for the glare. Her hearing was in no way impaired, though, which ensured that she had no trouble hearing the door opening and the sounds of other people entering the room. She squinted, the better to see.

Two men, a woman and a dog had come in, the oldest man in a wheelchair. Her grandfather, she presumed. The younger man must be Rafe — the dog appeared to be his — and the elderly woman, her great-aunt.

The man in the wheelchair was the first to speak. 'Delia said we had a rather interesting visitor.' He glanced casually at Christie and, despite being almost blinded by the sun, she couldn't miss his double-take. 'Oh, my word!' He'd clearly marked the likeness to his wife. 'Who's this? I didn't know . . . '

Venetia cut in. 'This, my dear Victor, is Christie. Our granddaughter — or so she claims. Adam and Laura's daughter.'

The old man gave a gasp. 'I think, my dear, that we must take her word for it. The likeness is . . . is . . . ' He seemed to run out of words then, but his gaze was warm and cheered Christie immensely. 'Well, what a wonderful surprise. We had no idea.'

The other two people who had come in were presumably too shocked to speak. They sat down in two of the remaining chairs and proceeded to scrutinize Christie in total silence.

Christie had just decided she'd better say something, make some sort of attempt to ease the tension of the situation, when the door opened once again and a man who bore no resemblance whatever to the other four people in the room walked in.

2

'Ah, Lucas,' Venetia greeted him, 'you're just in time for the introductions.'

Who on earth was Lucas? Christie wondered. Her mother hadn't mentioned him. Maybe he hadn't been here at the time that she and Adam had left? She supposed he could be Rafe's son — except that he didn't look anything like the older man. He also looked a few years older than her, which meant he would have had to have been born while her mother and Rafe were still married, wouldn't he? So, that would seem to rule that theory out. And he was way too young to be her great-aunt's . . .

'This is Christie,' Venetia told him. 'Adam and Laura's daughter — or so she says.'

Christie darted a glance back at her

grandmother. That sounded as if she didn't believe Christie despite their remarkable physical similarities.

'You didn't know them. However, I'm sure Rafe would have told you the story of how they left before you arrived.' Lucas simply nodded his confirmation of this statement. Rafe said nothing. Venetia then turned to look back at her granddaughter. 'Lucas — Lucas Grant to give him his full name — came to us at the age of ten. His mother was Victor's god-daughter. She and her husband both died in a car accident. As Lucas had no other relatives he came to live here and has remained with us ever since.'

'Venetia — ' Victor's tone betrayed his impatience with his wife. ' — never mind all that now. Tell us about — Christie, isn't it?' He smiled at Christie — a welcoming, tender smile, the sort of smile you expected from a grandfather.

Christie nodded, returning the smile with relief. If she counted Delia, that made two friends in this formidable house.

'I'm afraid I don't know any more than I've just told you, Victor,' Venetia said. 'Perhaps Christie would care to enlighten us.'

Everyone now turned their heads to look at Christie. She was beginning to feel like some sort of botanical specimen in the process of being minutely examined by a team of scientists, and highly sceptical scientists, at that.

She took a deep breath. 'Um . . . well, um . . . '

Nobody spoke, not even her grandfather.

She tried again. 'I-I didn't know about any of you either, I'm afraid.'

Her great-aunt gave a soft gasp and pressed a lace handkerchief to her lips.

'My-my mother, Laura, died recently.' Her eyes misted at the memory. 'But before she did, she told me I had a family. You.' She ventured a shaky smile. 'And she made me promise to seek you out. I think she-she was worried about me being left alone, which is a little silly at my age — I'm quite capable of taking care of myself.' She stopped talking abruptly. She was gabbling, as she had a tendency to do whenever she was nervous.

Her great-aunt sighed, frantically fluttering the handkerchief in front of her mouth as if in distress.

When nobody spoke, Christie continued, 'So . . . here I am.'

Christie could only conclude from the ensuing silence that they were all too shocked to speak. Either that, or they disapproved of her unannounced arrival. She gazed beseechingly at her grandmother, mutely pleading for her help. And surprisingly, given her up-til-then censorious and suspicious reaction to Christie's appearance at her door, she readily responded.

'Let me introduce everyone properly.' Venetia indicated Victor. 'Your grandfather, Victor — but I'm sure you've guessed that.' The old man again smiled encouragingly at her. 'Your uncle, Rafe.' She gestured towards the middle aged man. 'Your mother's first husband. I presume she told you she'd been married before?'

Christie nodded, unaccountably feeling that some sort of apology was due to Rafe, even though what had happened was in no way her fault. She hadn't even been born at the time. Nonetheless, she smiled remorsefully at him. Rafe gave no indication, however, that he'd seen her gesture. In fact, after the first few moments, when he'd given her a long, hard stare, he'd been at great pains, it seemed, not to glance her way. He seemed to be studying something through the window, something in the garden that required every bit of his attention.

'Your great-aunt Alice,' Venetia went on. 'My younger sister. She, too, lives here with us. And of course Lucas, whom I've already introduced. Now, have you any proof that you're who you say you are?'

The question, fired at her out of the blue as it was, shocked Christie. She'd thought her grandmother had finally accepted she was who she said she was. Over the past few minutes or so, she'd certainly been behaving as if she had. Clearly, however, she hadn't.

'Venetia! How can you doubt she's who she says she is? Look at her, for heaven's sake. She's the very image of you fifty, sixty years ago. Even today, you can see you're closely related.'

'Well, appearances can be misleading.' The old lady was clearly going to stick to her guns.

Christie opened her handbag. She'd come prepared for just this question. She'd brought the three letters that her grandmother had written to her father, plus her birth certificate. Silently, she handed them to her grandmother.

Venetia scanned them all briefly before handing them back. 'Thank you.'

Christie stowed them away again.

'Tell me, how did Laura die?' This was Victor speaking.

'Brain tumour. It was very quick; she didn't suffer for too long.' Her voice shook. She bit her bottom lip, telling herself she mustn't break down, not in front of these people. Such a display of weakness, although perfectly natural under such painful circumstances, would be humiliating.

'Oh dear, oh dear.' Victor sounded genuinely sorry. 'She must still have been relatively young.'

'Yes, she was. Too young,' Christie told him, thankful that she'd managed to suppress her grief. Family or not, to Christie they were still strangers.

Alice began to sniff into her handkerchief. 'For goodness sake, Alice,' Venetia began wearily, 'don't start snivelling. You haven't seen Laura for years.'

'It's Christie I'm crying for.' And indeed, the faded blue eyes were brimming with tears which she began to gently dab at with her scrap of lace. 'Oh dear. I feel quite faint at the thought of what you must have suffered, dear. Quite, quite faint.'

'Thank you,' Christie gratefully said. 'But, really, I'm okay.'

'Well — ' Venetia got to her feet. ' — you'll obviously stay here.'

'But — ' began Christie, getting to her feet as well, ' — I've taken a room at the Royal Oak.'

'Nonsense — you'll stay here. Collect your things and come straight back.'

'But I wasn't planning on staying long. I have to get home.' She really didn't want to stay here. She had become increasingly aware of Lucas's laser-like gaze. It was as if it were penetrating every part of her, uncovering her deepest feelings and thoughts. She didn't think it had left her from the moment he'd entered the room. He and Rafe were the only ones who still hadn't spoken. But they didn't need words; their hostility was tangible as it winged its way across the room towards her.

Were battle lines being drawn? she wondered. It certainly felt like it. But over what? She'd done nothing wrong, as far as she could tell. Well, apart from turning up on their doorstep, she supposed. But whatever the reason, she knew she couldn't stay. Still, she should have anticipated the invitation and had a plausible excuse ready; more plausible than 'I have to get home'. Couldn't she have done better than that? As a reason not to stay, it was downright pathetic.

'Job to go back to?' Lucas unexpectedly asked.

'No. I left my job.'

'Oh?' His eyes narrowed. 'And why is that?'

Was that suspicion she detected in his tone? It certainly sounded like it.

She stiffened. 'The company was taken over by a multi-national conglomerate a couple of months ago and I didn't wish to go on working for them. Too impersonal.' The cool words effectively concealed the pain she'd felt at losing both her job and her mother in the space of a few weeks, although the loss of her job had been her own decision entirely.

'So what will you do? I mean, you'll need an income — otherwise how will you support yourself?' His blunt words unmistakably implied that she shouldn't expect her grandparents to keep her. He was, she decided, warning her off. And then the reason for his barely disguised suspicion dawned. He thought she'd come to scrounge off them.

Furious at his insinuation, she snapped, 'I intend to have one. I'm planning on opening an art gallery.'

'Are you now? With what?' The question was fired at her.

'Wh-what do you mean?'

'Well, you'll need rather a large sum of money to do that.'

'Yes, and I'll have it — well, some of it. I'm an artist myself — or I like to think I am.' Her smile then was, she hoped, a confident as well as an untroubled one. 'So I aim to provide a large part of my stock myself.' She swung back to her grandmother. 'I'm not here in order to ask for anything. I've been left very well provided for, and apart from that, the sale of our house will bring a decent sum of money. The mortgage was practically paid off.'

'Oh?' Venetia sounded surprised.

'Yes. Both my parents proved rather good at playing the stock market. They made quite a lot of money between them, my mother especially. She seemed to have a natural aptitude.' She didn't look at Lucas, but he could have been in no doubt that her words were aimed specifically at him.

'I see.' A hint of something — Christie couldn't be sure but she rather thought it was pride in her son — flickered in Venetia's eyes. She glanced across at Lucas. 'That's okay then.' Her look quite clearly said, 'See, she's not here for mercenary reasons.' She'd also interpreted his veiled warning.

'Quite.' Rafe also spoke now for the very first time. 'Because let me tell you: right now, young lady, there's nothing here for you. Your father's treacherous behaviour made sure of that.' He bestowed a stare upon Christie that was brimful of contemptuous animosity.

* * *

45

Christie duly returned to the hotel and packed her belongings, which didn't take long as she hadn't brought much with her; and, with a feeling of deep apprehension, she returned to Heron House. Her grandmother had been adamant that she stay so, not wishing to upset the old lady, she had reluctantly agreed. She didn't plan to remain long in any case; just long enough to acquaint herself properly with her unknown family. A week at most, she decided. She could always visit again. Devon wasn't that far away from Worcestershire.

She needed to start organizing her gallery. She'd already found a small shop that could be altered without too much trouble to suit her purposes. It had a flat above, which meant she could live on the premises. It would, however, swallow up the better part of her inheritance, so she needed to start making some money. She hadn't been quite honest in her declaration that she was well provided for. Her mother had left some money, though nothing like the sizable amount she'd made it sound. The sale of the family home would help but it was only a small house in a terrace, so it wouldn't fetch that much. And, despite what she'd said, there was still a mortgage on it; it wasn't a lot but it would have to be paid out of whatever she got for it.

She didn't know what had come over her. She wasn't usually deceitful, but Lucas's insinuation that she wanted something — money, presumably — from her grandparents had incensed her, making her throw caution to the winds and vastly exaggerate her financial situation.

Before she vacated her room, however, there were a couple more things she needed to do. She used her mobile phone firstly to ring Toby. She was beginning to wish with all her heart that she'd done as he'd wanted and let him come with her. He worked for the same firm as Christie, Pringle's Engineering — now Bristow's in the wake of the takeover — but, as opposed to Christie's decision to leave her position as deputy head of the accounts office, he was remaining. As a potential departmental manager, he foresaw a rosy future. But it also meant that with the new people only just in place, he couldn't suddenly ask for extra time off — not yet, even though he'd clearly been prepared to do just that.

But now she found herself wondering whether his presence might have deflected suspicion of her motives for being here, although quite how it would have done that she didn't know. One thing it would have done, though, was bolster her spirit; her fortitude — something she felt desperately in need of right now.

Even so, the manner in which Lucas had regarded her, and Rafe had spoken to her, made her doubt that anything or anyone would have changed things. They had it set in their minds that she was after whatever she could get and that was that. Case closed.

48

'Toby,' she now said, 'it's Christie.'

'Christie! I was going to ring you later. How are things? Okay?'

He still sounded anxious about her, but then he was a bit of a worrier. Christie smiled to herself. He'd be a loving, considerate partner — husband — she was sure of that. So why couldn't she commit herself to him?

'Yes, I'm fine. I'm moving out of the hotel.'

'Aah.' His tone told her that he'd already anticipated that.

'My grandmother insists that I stay at Heron House.'

'Well, I can't say I'm surprised. A previously unknown granddaughter turning up out of the blue — they're bound to want to get to know you better. What are they like?'

'Unusual.'

'Unusual? In what way?' Toby's tone sharpened.

'Well, my grandmother is obviously the matriarch of the family. I can see why my father deemed her bossy. I

49

sense she likes things her own way. But on the plus side, my grandfather is a darling, as is my great-aunt Alice. My uncle Rafe . . . ' She paused.

'What about your Uncle Rafe?'

'He's not very . . . welcoming, shall we say. In fact, he's positively hostile.'

'That's it, I'm coming down. You shouldn't be on your own.'

'Toby, I'm fine. Honestly.'

'You don't sound it.'

'I know, but there's-there's someone else living there . . . ' Again she hesitated.

'Who?' The single word exploded with all the ferocity and speed of a bullet fired from a high-calibre weapon.

'A man called Lucas Grant. He's the son of my grandfather's goddaughter. His parents were both killed when he was a boy. My grandparents took him in. He's . . . '

How to describe Lucas? If she told Toby the truth — that he, as well as Rafe, displayed only suspicion and dislike; contempt, even; so much so, in fact, that she'd begun to feel as if she were under siege — he'd be down there by the end of the day. And that, she realized, she didn't want, despite her earlier reflections.

'What, Christie? For heaven's sake, tell me. What is he?'

'Shall we say, he's a bit distrustful too.'

'Distrustful of you?'

Christie gave a short laugh. 'Yeah. He thinks I'm after something. Money, I presume. As, I suspect, does Uncle Rafe.'

'Enough said,' Toby burst out. 'You clearly need support. I'll be there by tomorrow lunchtime. There are a couple of things I must sort out here first.'

She sighed. He was reacting just as she'd feared. Why hadn't she kept her mouth shut? Why did she always have to say just that bit too much? If Toby turned up, Lucas and Rafe would assume they had two scroungers on their hands instead of just one.

'No, Toby — please. You can't take extra time off now, you know that. I'll be fine. Really. There's absolutely nothing to worry about and, frankly, you also turning up out of the blue immediately after me stands a very good chance of simply making matters even worse. They'd probably think we're working in cahoots. Look, I've got to go. I'll ring you again.'

'Make sure you do. Tomorrow, Christie. Ring me tomorrow.'

* * *

Her next call was to her closest and dearest friend Saffie, short for Saffron. She always claimed her mother had had some sort of brainstorm when choosing a name for her — never mind that she'd always loved the colour. That was no excuse in Saffie's mind for saddling her with such an outlandish appellation. 'Thank God her favourite colour isn't navy blue,' Saffie was fond of crying, and Christie had to agree. Saffron was bad enough; imagine being called Navy Blue! Not surprisingly, at the age of eight her friend had decided to shorten it to what she had decided was a more acceptable name, and so she became known for ever afterwards as Saffie — much to her mother's annoyance.

Saffie and Christie had been close friends since junior school. So close, in fact, that she felt like the sister Christie had never had. There was nothing she wouldn't tell Saffie, which was why she desperately needed to ring her now — to unburden herself and hopefully gain some sort of reassurance, as well as a much-needed perspective on it all. Saffie had always been great at that sort of thing. She didn't know the meaning of the word 'panic'. Mind you, during their schooldays she'd also been great at leading Christie into all sorts of trouble, once even putting them at risk of expulsion. But she did have the knack of being able to view things from a more positive angle than Christie. Nothing got Saffie down. Nothing. She was one of those people whose glass was always half-full.

'Saffie, it's me.'

'Christie — I've been waiting to hear from you. How're things down in deepest Devon?'

'Okay.'

'Oh, only okay?'

'Afraid so.'

'Oh — good grief, they didn't refuse to let you in, did they?'

'No, far from it. They've asked me to stay at the house.'

'But you must have expected that, surely?'

'I suppose so.'

'Well, what's wrong then? Because clearly something is.'

'We-ell, my grandfather's great,' she began, 'and my grandmother . . . ' She repeated what she'd already told Toby.

'Okay . . . ' Saffie waited for her to go on.

'My great-aunt Alice, on the other hand, waves a lace hankie all over the place, for all the world like some sort of

54

demure Victorian maiden. I keep expecting her to have a fit of the vapours.'

This induced a chuckle from Saffie.

'And then, there's Uncle Rafe,' Christie paused.

'Go on then. What about Uncle Rafe?'

'Well, you're right, there is something wrong. He's what's wrong. He wasn't at all pleased to see me and made it very obvious. In fact, he seems to blame me, you know, for Mum leaving.' She'd told Saffie everything that her mother had told her and had even shown her the letters. 'He's certainly resentful of me and not bothering to hide it. In fact, so far all he's said to me is that there's nothing here for me. I assume he means money.'

'Oh dear. So you won't be playing Happy Families then?'

'Not as far as he's concerned, no. But there's someone else here — a man called Lucas Grant, the son of my grandfather's god-daughter. He's lived with the family since he was ten apparently, when both his parents were killed. And he, too, seems to think I'm only here for what I can get out of my grandparents. He all but warned me off.'

'Flippin' cheek! Who does he think he is?'

'The favourite grandson from all appearances.'

'You do sound a bit beleaguered by it all.' As usual Saffie was spot-on. 'Do you want me to come down — for a spot of moral support, if nothing else? Because I will — '

For a minute she was tempted, but then practicality clicked in. 'No, no, course not. Toby's already offered and as I told him, another arrival would only make Lucas think they'd got landed with two scroungers instead of just one.'

'Blow Lucas. It's nothing to do with him.'

'The trouble is, I have an uneasy suspicion he thinks it's everything to do with him. In fact, I'm beginning to think he's appointed himself the family's legal and financial guardian.'

When Christie eventually returned to the house, it was to find it deserted — apart from Delia, that was.

'Where is everybody?' she asked as she followed the housekeeper up the stairs to her room.

'We-ell, your grandparents usually have a rest in the afternoon. Your uncle Rafe has gone out . . . ' There was an infinitesimal pause, almost as if she were about to say more then decided not to. 'Your aunt is having her afternoon walk, and Lucas is probably off somewhere working.'

A sensation of relief engulfed Christie. She'd have some time to settle herself in and have a look round before having to meet the family again; have time to prepare herself for further hostilities, even. She'd glimpsed what had looked like superb gardens as she'd arrived and was longing to go and have a look. She would surely discover a subject or two

57

for some paintings. She'd decided she may as well occupy herself productively while she was here. She needed some more paintings for her gallery, so she'd brought all her materials with her just in case.

Delia showed her into a huge bedroom, complete with a magnificent four-poster bed and her own huge marble-tiled en-suite bathroom, before saying, 'Dinner will be served at six o'clock. The old people don't like to eat too late. Now, is there anything I can get you before then?'

'No, thank you. I'll unpack and maybe have a look round — get my bearings, if that's all right?'

★　★　★

So that was what she did. It took her mere moments to stash her few belongings away in the massive antique wardrobe and matching chest of drawers. After which she grabbed a sweater — as her grandmother had already pointed out, the day wasn't as warm as one might expect for June — and ran down the sweeping staircase to have her much-anticipated look around.

The house was pretty impressive, with rooms tucked away everywhere. Besides the library, which she'd already seen, there was a large elegantly furnished drawing room and an equally elegant dining room, its walls hung with portraits of family members — everyone except her parents, that was. There was a small sitting room — did they call it a snug? She wasn't sure. There was what she assumed was a breakfast room with a pine table and chairs; a kitchen, of course, which also was empty — Delia, too, must be having a rest; a butler's pantry, judging by the sheer amount of china and glasses stacked on shelves; a separate larder; a fully equipped laundry room . . . the list went on and on.

Eventually she wandered back into the hallway, and from there went outside. If the house had been impressive, the gardens were spectacular: there were sweeping and immaculately mown lawns; winding paths; several large, well-stocked flower beds and borders; a hedged garden; a large lake — her fingers itched to hold a paintbrush. Maybe tomorrow? For now, she simply wished to get a feel for the place.

She spotted Alice on the far side of the lake. She waved but the older woman couldn't have seen her because she didn't respond.

★ ★ ★

Dinner that evening proved a fairly tense affair. Christie had dressed in a pair of cream cotton cropped trousers and a T-shirt. She was slightly dismayed, therefore, to see her grandmother in a long formal skirt and frilly blouse, and her grandfather in a lightweight suit. Aunt Alice was marginally more casual in a mid-calf-length dress. Lucas and Rafe were both attired in open-necked shirts and perfectly tailored trousers. Christie felt both underdressed and embarrassed.

No one seemed to notice, however, so gradually she relaxed. She didn't talk much, preferring to listen and learn more of these relatives of hers. One thing she did observe was how very close Rafe and Lucas were, Lucas treating the older man with all the deference and fondness of a son for a father. Maybe Lucas regarded Rafe as a substitute for his dead father?

To her disappointment though, conversation was pretty general, so Christie failed to glean much in the way of personal information about any of them. She did become aware, though, of Lucas's narrowed gaze resting upon her with increasing frequency. Was he still suspicious of her motives for coming here, despite her statement concerning the financial health of her situation? Maybe he'd seen through her duplicity? If his perceptive abilities were any match for his penetrating stare, then she wouldn't be at all surprised.

Eventually he asked, 'What sort of painting do you do?'

'Still life. Landscapes. I've even been known to paint the odd portrait or two.'

'Really?' Alice clasped her two hands together against her chest, lace handkerchief fluttering as she did so. She must have been quite beautiful once, Christie decided. The evidence was still there in the high cheekbones and fine bone structure of her face. Even her lips had retained much of the fullness of a younger woman. 'Could you paint us?' she went on in the excited tones of a young girl. 'All of us?' She spoke as if she were soliciting some sort of treat.

'All of you?' Christie echoed in some dismay. How long was she expected to stay here? To paint all of them would take several weeks; months, even.

'Yes, you know, a family group.'

'Don't be ridiculous, Alice,' Venetia interrupted. 'Why would she want to waste her time doing that? The girl needs to paint for payment, not out of charity.'

'Well, we could pay her.' Alice's cheeks were pink with excitement now, and her blue eyes glistened, their faded colour deepening dramatically — almost feverishly — as she turned to Victor and beseeched, 'Couldn't we?'

'No.' Venetia's implacable tone effectively put an end to that line of conversation. 'When do you envisage your gallery opening?'

'Well, depending on how much needs doing with the premises that I've found — '

'Oh — ' Lucas's interest sharpened. ' — you've found a place then?'

'Yes.'

'Where?'

'Linford Green.'

'Where's that?'

'Worcestershire, where I live.'

'I've never heard of Linford Green.'

'Why would you have?'

He ignored this display of defiance. 'Wouldn't you do better in a city?'

Resentment stirred in her breast at the questions being fired practically non-stop at her. Who on earth did he think he was, to interrogate her in such a fashion? He wasn't even a real member of the family; he was a guest. A long-term guest, it was true, but nonetheless just a guest.

As a consequence of her vexation with him, her response was terse. 'Not really. The expenses would be too high — presuming I could afford to buy a city centre shop in the first place.'

'Oh.' He raised an eyebrow. 'I thought you'd been left a substantial inheritance — ?'

Christie gnawed at her bottom lip. He'd picked up on her unintentional slip. Yet again, she'd blurted out too much — when was she ever going to learn? And now he knew, or suspected at the very least, that she'd embellished her circumstances; lied, even. Which, of course, she had — but he'd made her so angry with his insinuation that she was only here to scrounge off her grandparents, that she hadn't been able to help herself. Still, she shouldn't have succumbed to such misguided temptation. All she could do now was try to bluff her way out of the situation she'd so impetuously landed herself in.

'Well,' she began, 'I may have given the wrong impression. My inheritance wasn't that substantial; certainly not substantial enough to subsidise a city-centre shop.' Ignoring his expression of what she interpreted as righteous satisfaction — he was obviously convinced that his theory about her precipitate arrival was the correct one, and she was here to scrounge off her grandparents — she turned to ask her uncle, 'And you, Uncle Rafe — what do you do?'

Her grandmother gave a snort. 'As little as possible.'

Rafe instantly and angrily retaliated. 'Mother! It's not my fault I can't find gainful employment. No one wants people over the age of fifty anymore, never mind sixty.'

'When was the last time you worked, Rafe?' she demanded.

Christie fidgeted in her seat. A family row was the very last thing she'd intended. But how could she have known what sort of reaction her guileless question would provoke?

'We-ell . . . ' Rafe also began to fidget. 'I can't exactly recall.'

'Precisely,' Venetia retaliated. 'It's too long ago to remember.'

'Venetia, there's no need to pick on Rafe,' Alice protested.

Venetia ignored her and instead picked up a spoon and banged it on the table for silence. Not that anyone was talking. The entire company had fallen into a somewhat uncomfortable silence.

Christie felt a giggle of hysteria start up in her throat, something else she was prone to do in times of stress. She swallowed hard, forcibly suppressing the urge. Lord, was dinner like this every night? No wonder her parents had chosen to leave. Venetia would most likely have made their lives extremely difficult, especially in the event of Christie's birth. She could understand now why her father had feared his mother's interference. Command came naturally to her. What was not so clear was why the rest of the family allowed her to behave in such a dictatorial fashion. Other than Rafe, no one seemed prepared to argue with her. Would she be expected to toe Venetia's line, too, while she was here? And what would happen if she refused?

Venetia began to speak. 'Victor and I have something to tell you all.' All eyes turned to Venetia. 'Victor,' she said, 'do you want to tell them?'

'No, dear, you're much better at this sort of thing than me.' Victor thus confirmed Christie's instinct about her grandmother being very much the matriarch.

Venetia smiled at him, inclining her head slightly, graciously accepting the inevitable. 'Thank you. Now, obviously Christie's unexpected arrival has dramatically altered the existing situation.'

Suddenly, everyone was sitting more upright. Christie smothered another giggle. She half-expected them all to leap to their feet, clicking their heels together to salute her grandmother in true military fashion.

'So, with the thought that Victor's and my deaths can't be far ahead, we will, of course, be altering our will — '

It was Christie's turn now to sit up straighter, as a sensation of pure dread engulfed her.

' — to take our granddaughter's existence into account.'

'Oh no, please, no,' she began. 'That wasn't why I came.'

'Oh, was it not?' Rafe glared at her. 'You do surprise me.'

Christie didn't dare look at Lucas, for fear of what she would see on his face.

'Be quiet, Rafe. Now — ' Venetia glanced haughtily at the other people around the table. ' — naturally, whichever one of us dies first will leave everything to the other. But upon the death of the survivor, Christie will receive half of everything as our only grandchild. She will, in fact, get what Adam would have had if he had lived and returned home. The other half will go to Rafe. Obviously before it is split in two, there will be smaller bequests to other members of the family — namely, Alice and Lucas. Alice will, of course, be allowed to live out her life here at Heron House. As will Lucas, should he so desire.'

3

For an endless moment, no one said anything; not a word. As for Christie, she couldn't have spoken if her life had depended on it. This was the last thing she'd expected or wanted. She'd rather have been turned away than to be listening to such an announcement.

It was Rafe who eventually broke the silence. 'So she turns up, out of the blue, after keeping her existence a complete secret for what, twenty years?'

'Twenty-four,' Christie bit out. She'd never before been on the receiving end of such open dislike, and she couldn't help but think, if only her mother hadn't told her about this previously unknown family; hadn't made her promise to come here. If she hadn't, no one would have known of her existence, and she could have carried on with her life, unaware that these people even existed.

Yet, Laura hadn't been stupid. She must have had some inkling that Christie would meet with this sort of — distrustful hostility? Or had she hoped that the passing years would have mellowed old emotions and hatreds, making long-ago events seem insignificant; acceptable, even? If she had, she couldn't have been more wrong, certainly with regards to Rafe. She clearly hadn't known about Lucas. Now it turned out that Laura had heedlessly thrown her only daughter to a pair of ravening wolves. At least, that was how it felt.

' . . . and gets handed virtually half of everything. Is that really fair, Mother? Father? I mean, what does that mean for me? Me, who's stayed here with you both throughout everything.' He threw his napkin onto the table and lurched to his feet.

'Sit down, Rafe.' Venetia sounded as if she were only too accustomed to this sort of scene; was resigned to it, in fact. Wearily so.

Surprisingly, Rafe did as he was commanded. Or rather, he slumped rather than sat. Christie had expected further heated protest; a full-blown family row, even.

'You would only have got the same if Adam had stayed, Rafe,' Venetia continued.

'Yes, but Adam didn't stay, did he?' he once more burst out. 'He ran off with my wife, for God's sake. Doesn't that mean anything to you? Don't I deserve more?'

'If you'd been a better husband, Rafe, undoubtedly Laura would have stayed with you. You brought it on yourself. Now then, Victor — ' Her tone signalled that this was the end of that particular discussion. ' — you're looking tired. Lucas, would you carry him upstairs, please?'

Rafe, looking thoroughly defeated, stayed silent. Christie, on the other hand, couldn't. She had to say something, make some sort of protest. Rafe had a valid point. This division of the inheritance simply wasn't fair. She couldn't possibly accept it. 'Grandmother — ' she began.

'Yes?' Venetia turned an untroubled gaze upon her. It was as if the argument with her son had never happened.

'Please, there's no need for you to do this. I wasn't expecting — '

There was a low snort of what sounded like pure cynicism from across the room. Whether it came from Rafe or Lucas she couldn't have said, and she had no intention of looking their way to find out.

'Christie, it's what you're entitled to,' Venetia insisted.

'No. As Rafe has said, I've just turned up — out of the blue.'

'Fortunately.' Venetia unexpectedly smiled at her. At least her grandparents had accepted her, wholeheartedly. That thought went some way towards consoling her, even in the face of Rafe's unmitigated hatred.

'It's not fair.'

'Fair!' her grandmother echoed. 'Of course it's fair. You're our only grandchild. I want to hear nothing more about it. Our minds are quite made up.'

And that was that. Christie was effectively silenced.

She sank back into her chair. Had her mother expected this to happen? Was that why she'd made Christie promise to come? To ensure that her daughter would be well provided for?

Once Victor, Venetia and Lucas had left the room, an uncomfortable silence descended upon the three remaining people. Alice hadn't said a word throughout, but now she too stood up.

'Well, I'm exhausted. I shall leave you to go to my bed also.'

She did look very pale. The evening's events had obviously taken their toll. Belatedly, she looked like the elderly woman she was.

'Aunt Alice, can't you speak to Grandmother?' Christie pleaded. 'Persuade her that it's wrong to leave half of everything to me?'

'My dear, there's something that you will have to understand. My sister has always been a law unto herself. If she's decided that that's what's going to happen,

74

then that's what will happen. She certainly won't listen to anything that I say. Never has, never will.' She gave an absent smile, patting her lips with the lacy handkerchief that she seemed to keep permanently at the ready. 'Rafe, dear, would you escort me to my room?'

Rafe got to his feet. Once more, he took great care not to glance Christie's way. Frightened of what he might be driven to say to her now that his mother had gone? All of this strife was the very last thing Christie had expected when she'd arrived here. She'd thought her grandparents might refuse to recognize her, but this bitterness — hatred — on the part of her uncle towards her, who hadn't even been born at the time of Laura's desertion and so had been in no way involved . . . No, she certainly hadn't expected that. And now that emotion had been exacerbated by her grandmother's actions.

'I'll see you in the morning, Christie,' the old woman said. 'Tell me, is that your real name?'

'Yes — well, it's Christina actually, but everyone has always called me Christie and it's what I prefer.'

'I see. Well, goodnight, dear. Sleep well.'

★   ★   ★

Despite her great-aunt's bidding, it took Christie a considerable time to get to sleep that night, and when she finally did it was to be almost immediately woken by the opening of her bedroom door — or at least, she thought the door opened. When she turned her head to see who had entered the room, no one was there, and in the darkness the door appeared still closed.

She reached out and switched on the bedside light. Had someone looked in on her? Her grandmother, maybe? It couldn't be anyone else, could it? Nervously, she sat up and listened; when she heard nothing, she climbed out of bed and crept to the door. She'd definitely closed it behind her, so . . . Yes, it was very slightly open. She closed it once more, firmly — just as a floorboard creaked on the landing outside.

Someone was out there.

She swept a glance towards the clock on her bedside table. It was almost three o'clock. Who on earth was wandering around at this hour? She cracked the door open again and put an eye to the gap. The landing was in total darkness. There wasn't even any moonlight to illuminate whoever might be prowling about.

She opened the door wider and stuck her head out. She caught the faintest of movements from the corner of her eye, right where the landing formed a right angle, leading to the stairs down as well as several more bedrooms.

'Grandmother?' Christie softly called. 'Is that you?'

Slowly, silently, she crept to where she'd thought she'd seen something — someone? She peered round the corner but there was no one there; nothing moved and there was no sound at all, apart from the loud ticking of the grandfather clock that stood in the hallway.

Thoughtfully, she walked back to her room. Had someone been there, someone who'd opened her bedroom door and looked in on her as she lay sleeping? She wrapped her arms about herself and shivered. Suddenly she was full of misgivings about this house and its inhabitants.

Which was ridiculous. They were her family. They wouldn't hurt her — would they?

Still, she couldn't rid herself of the notion that someone had looked into her room. And if she was right, who had it been? And more to the point, why? The only explanation she could come up with was the one she'd already considered: that it had been Venetia. Maybe she was afraid that Christie would disappear again as precipitately as she had arrived?

Eventually she did sleep again, only to wake much later than she had intended; as a consequence, she felt heavy-headed and slightly unwell. Part of which was probably due, she decided, to the shock of the previous evening, when she'd learnt that she was to be left nearly half of everything that the Wakehams possessed. A very considerable amount, she guessed, judging by the fuss that Rafe was making.

However, upon drawing back her bedroom curtains, the warmth of the sun upon her face and the sight of unbroken blue of the sky was more than enough to cheer her. She pushed the window open and leant out. The air felt warmer than the day before; considerably warmer. Her spirits lifted.

The scent of roses drifted towards her, and — she sniffed — yes, honeysuckle. She looked down. There was a huge splash of both right beneath her, the honeysuckle rambling unchecked through the rose as it clambered up the wall, the fragrant blossoms of both a magnet for the dozens of bees that were weaving their amongst the flowers as they busily and noisily gathered the nectar. She wondered if there were any hives in the grounds. It would explain this number of bees and it would make sense to produce one's own honey. They probably had done years ago.

Kraak, Kraak. A heron — the same one as yesterday? she wondered — flew over. She gazed upwards, fervently wishing she could do the same and simply fly away. Maybe she should escape the house for a while and give everyone's emotions time to calm down. Allow the various occupants of the house to come to terms with her presence, albeit a temporary one. She'd take her watercolour paints and get on with some work.

Inspired with the notion of indulging herself with a pastime that she loved, and which hopefully was going to furnish her with a decent income, she swiftly showered and pulled on a pair of cropped jeans and a T-shirt. She'd banished from her mind the disturbing possibility of someone having entered her room the night before. She'd consider the implications of it later; maybe ask her grandmother if it had been her. Perhaps the old lady, excited by the arrival of a completely unknown granddaughter, had been unable to sleep. Maybe she'd wanted to check that Christie had really been there and it hadn't all been simply a dream. Because, if there had been an intruder, who else could it have been? Rafe? Lucas? Either seemed highly improbable, since catching a man — any man — peeking into her bedroom could leave him open to all sort of accusations, not least that of salacious voyeurism. And it couldn't have been her grandfather; he needed a wheelchair to get around. That only left her elderly aunt and her grandmother. Of those two, the most likely candidate was Venetia.

*　*　*

Feeling more reassured in the wake of her deductions, she gathered together everything that she'd need and left her room to make her way along the landing and down the stairs into the hallway. On her earlier exploration she'd discovered a door that led directly from the kitchen into the garden at the rear of the house, and that was where she found Delia industriously preparing lunch.

'Good morning,' the housekeeper said, smiling warmly.

Christie smiled back. 'Something smells good.'

'Chicken salad. I hope you like it.'

Christie nodded. 'Although I probably won't be here to enjoy it. I thought I'd take myself off for the day and do some painting. I've brought my materials with me.'

'What a good idea. You'll find plenty of lovely views.'

'Do you know where my grand-parents are?'

'Mrs Wakeham is in the small sitting room attending to some correspondence. Mr Wakeham, I believe, is still in their bedroom. I gather he's rather tired after the excitement of your arrival yesterday. Not surprising, really. He's not strong, I'm afraid.'

'Oh dear. Should I go and see him?'

'I wouldn't. He's probably asleep

still. He'll be down later, I'm sure. You go out and enjoy yourself.'

'I'll just find my grandmother and let her know what I'm doing.'

'And I'll prepare you a cold lunch to take with you, as you missed breakfast. Something to keep you going till supper.'

Christie poked her head around the door of the sitting room and saw her grandmother at a small ornately crafted desk, busily writing on a notepad. She went into the room and said, 'I just wanted to say, Grandmother, I'm going out for a while, if that's okay.'

'Of course it's okay. Your grandfather and I are planning a quiet day.'

Christie paused and then said, 'Um . . . ' How to put this without giving offence? ' . . . you didn't look in on me last night, did you? Late last night?'

The old woman looked at her in surprise. 'Certainly not. Why on earth would I?'

'It's just that I thought someone did.'

'Well, did you not see who it was?'

'No. When I checked the door

— which I'm positive I'd closed — it was slightly ajar.'

'Well, maybe you hadn't closed it properly.' And Venetia turned her attention back to whatever it was she was writing. She clearly didn't believe there was anything to worry about.

'No, maybe I didn't.' It seemed easiest to go along with her grandmother's theory. And maybe she hadn't closed the door as securely as she'd thought and a current of air had cracked it open. After all, these old houses could be extremely draughty — this one more than most, if you took into account the sheer number of windows. Some of them were bound to have been left open on a summer's night; hers certainly had. But that didn't explain the creaking of the floorboards and the fact that she thought she saw something — something that disappeared almost at once.

Venetia turned back to her letter.

'Is Grandfather all right?'

'He's just tired.' Venetia was already

writing again. 'Nothing to concern yourself about.'

Christie felt dismissed, although she was sure her grandmother hadn't intended that. She quickly returned to the kitchen and picked up the lunch that Delia had prepared for her — a packet of chicken salad sandwiches and an apple, as well as a flask of coffee — and left the house. She wanted to paint the view across the lake, looking towards a picturesque summer house.

When she got to the spot, however, it was to discover her great-aunt already there, sitting on a wooden bench in the warm sunshine.

'Good morning, Christie,' she said. 'How are you? Did you sleep well?'

'Not really.' She paused, but then, despite having decided to dismiss the whole incident as a product of an overtired mind as well as an overactive imagination, was unable to prevent herself from doing another spot of probing. 'I thought someone looked into my room in the early hours. It woke me.'

Alice glanced up, looking as surprised as her sister had been. 'Goodness me. Are you sure you didn't dream it? I can't imagine anyone wandering around the house at night, opening bedroom doors.'

That hadn't occurred to her, that she'd been dreaming. But she hadn't been dreaming all of the time; she'd been wide awake. At least, she thought she had been. 'Maybe that was it, but — '

'I'm sure that's what it was, dear. Now, what are your plans for today?'

Christie told her.

'Oh, how lovely.' Just as she had the previous day, she clasped her hands to her mouth, the lace hankie that seemed to be permanently at the ready fluttering exactly as it had done then. She was child-like in her pleasure. Christie smiled at her, just as fondly as she would have done at a young girl.

'I'd love to watch you work. Would you mind?'

'No, of course not. In fact, it would be nice to have some company. All I need now is for the heron that I saw to fly over — or even better, land and stand over there.' Christie pointed to the reed-fringed bank opposite.

Alice's response was instantaneous and dramatic — and totally unexpected. Her face whitened as she pressed the scrap of lace even harder to her lips; her gasp was long and heartfelt. It was as if she were drawing every scrap of air that surrounded her directly into her lungs. Christie almost expected her to explode right there in front of her. Her chest, already generously proportioned, notice-ably expanded by several inches.

'Aunt Alice,' Christie said, 'are you all right?'

She didn't resemble a young girl now; in fact, she seemed to have aged years in just a matter of seconds. Every wrinkle, every deep line, was vividly etched upon her face. 'The-the heron that you saw?' For once the handkerchief was still, clasped tightly as she pressed her two small hands to her breast. 'Wh-what do you mean, dear? We haven't had herons here for years. Not since I was . . . oh dear, I can't remember when. I was just a girl. We used to have several of them, quite a colony. Are you sure it was a heron that you saw, Christie?' Her expression now was a fearful one.

'Oh, yes. Maybe they've come back. Twice I've seen one.'

There was another gasp. 'Oh dear. What can it mean?'

'Does it have to mean anything?' Christie began to unpack her paints, brushes and sketchpad.

'Oh yes. The last couple of times that one was seen — after a gap of many, many years, I might add — we had deaths in the family right afterwards.'

Christie stopped what she was doing and stared at her in amazement. She couldn't mean what that sounded like. 'What?'

'Yes, the sight of a heron came to be regarded as an ill omen; a harbinger of death. The first time was my and Venetia's mother. She fell down the stairs and broke her neck. The second

— quite a while later — was an uncle who was staying here. He drowned in this very lake. Each time, a heron had been sighted just hours before. Then they simply disappeared again.'

'But, surely you can't assume the deaths had anything to do with the appearance of a heron? I mean, it must have been coincidence.' And surely, she mused, herons must visit a lake this substantial on a regular basis. There were probably dozens of fish in it. No, the truth must be that Alice had never been here at the right time to see one.

'We-ell,' the old lady whispered, 'I hope so. I really do.'

Christie patted Alice's hand, trying to reassure her. She did look very frightened. Her lips were trembling, her hands shaking. Her eyes were like saucers in her still-ashen face. 'I'm sure that's all it was. Things like that simply don't happen. Now — ' Anxious to wipe the expression of alarm from her great-aunt's face, Christie sought to distract her. ' — tell me all about the

89

family. Lucas, for example. How long has he lived here?'

Her tactic worked. Alice's expression lightened, although it was obvious that she totally believed in her preposterous theory. 'Dear Lucas. Such a sweet boy.'

Boy? Christie mused. And sweet? That was like calling a man-eating tiger cuddly.

'He's lived here for twenty years now. He was ten when he arrived.'

Which made him thirty; hardly a boy.

'He was deeply unhappy, losing his parents at such a young age and in such tragic circumstances. He's grown very close to Rafe over the years.' She smiled serenely, all thoughts of impending tragedy clearly forgotten. 'He'd do anything for him, anything at all. He has his own apartment, of course, within the house. He needs to be independent at his age. He has a sitting room, bedroom, bathroom, even his own kitchen — all very luxurious and done at his own expense, naturally, although he mostly eats with the rest of us. He likes to do that. He insists on paying rent, though, and his own living costs. He's adamant about that, although it suits everyone to have him staying here. When he's at home he helps with Victor. In fact, I don't know what Venetia would do without him at times. I think that's why he's stayed.'

'What does he do?'

'Do, dear?' Alice looked confused.

'Yes. His work. What does he do?'

'Oh, I see. Well, now . . . What does he do?' She placed a finger on her lips and gave the question due thought. 'Oh, of course. How silly of me. He has his own business. Well, several actually.'

'Really? In what field?'

'Oh, dear me, I don't . . . ' The handkerchief fluttered. 'Engineering. Yes, that's it, engineering is one. And he's also big in construction, I think. Yes, he built the new leisure centre on the outskirts of Plymouth. He does lots of things. He's quite the entrepreneur.'

Christie wondered if she was quite as mentally alert as her sister. The occasional girlish — even child-like — behaviour could point to some sort of senility, or at least the beginnings of it. 'And you're the younger sister, didn't Grandmother say?' Christie knew very well she was — Venetia had introduced her as 'my younger sister' — but Christie wanted to keep her mind off the possible appearance of a heron, especially as one had fulfilled her desire and landed amongst the reeds immediately opposite. If her great-aunt should spot it, she would probably descend into hysterics.

Once again the tactic worked, because Alice smiled serenely and said, 'Yes. By two years. Venetia's eighty; I'm seventy eight. Although people always say that I look a lot younger.' And she smiled again, this time glancing up through lowered eyelashes. Christie couldn't help grinning. Who did she think she was, Princess Diana? 'Venetia's always looked after me, always organized me. I'm not very good.'

But then, unexpectedly, her eyes took on a faraway look, as if something had distracted her. She was staring over Christie's shoulder. Christie turned her head to see for herself what it was, but there was nothing and no one there. And she found herself wondering if Alice's mind was beginning to deteriorate. She did seem mentally erratic, and it was more than just the normal absent-mindedness that the elderly can sometimes suffer from. The question seemed to be answered when just a moment later Alice stood up and, without another word, wandered away, her request to watch Christie work evidently forgotten.

4

From then on, Christie's nights were undisturbed. She decided to forget all about the earlier incident. If it had been her grandmother checking on her — and she chose to think that it had been — then clearly the old lady wasn't going to admit to it. She would certainly view it as some sort of character weakness or defect.

However, one thing her grandmother made no secret of was her hope that Christie and Lucas might make a match of things. She regularly and frequently attempted to leave them in a room alone together, which proved mortifyingly embarrassing to Christie. Did she have to make it so obvious? Especially as Lucas was the very last man she was likely to be attracted to, having made no attempt to disguise his suspicions of her motives for being here at Heron House.

But apart from that aspect of things, he was altogether too good-looking for her taste; too sure of himself by half. She'd been hurt and humiliated by such men more than once. They were almost always self-obsessed and conceited. And usually untrustworthy. So now, with the precious benefit of hindsight, she repeated to herself 'several times bitten, many times shy' and she fully intended to stick with that philosophy. Lucas, who saw through Venetia's antics with as much clarity as Christie, merely looked amused by it all, before excusing himself and making an exit.

So she was considerably surprised when a couple of mornings later she met him on his way out of the house and he said, 'Shall we make an old woman very happy and go out together this evening?' His eyes glittered with the flecks of amber that she'd noticed on their first encounter.

'I don't go out with anyone just to make someone else happy,' she waspishly bit back. She was tempted to add, 'I'd rather chew my arm off,' but lost her nerve at the last minute.

'Not even your newly discovered grandmother?' he drily asked.

'No, not even my grandmother.'

'Okay.' He didn't look at all put out by her refusal. Which made her wonder just how sincere his invitation had been.

'I just thought — ' He shrugged his shoulders. So, Christie decided, she was right — he didn't care whether she went out with him or not. ' — it would be nice to get to know each other a little better. After all, we could eventually end up all living here together if Venetia has her way.'

Christie raised an eyebrow at him. Not if she had anything to do with it. And why suddenly ask her out now? Until this moment he'd made little or no effort to get to know her better. He'd eaten dinner with the family, it was true, but then had usually managed to escape, whether to his own apartment or to go out she had no idea. And frankly she didn't care either way. But

could it be that his invitation was some
sort of tactic to enable him to discover
what her plans were with regard to the
family? Find out whether she really was
only after whatever money there was to
be had? Or could Rafe have put him up
to it? What was it Alice had said? Lucas
would do anything for Rafe, anything
at all. So did that mean he'd go as far
as asking out a woman he had no
romantic interest in, simply to discover
what her intentions were?

'I won't be coming here to live on a
permanent basis. I have my own life
back in Worcestershire and I fully
intend to go on with it there.'

'I have to tell you, Christie, your
grandmother invariably gets her way.'

'Not this time.'

He studied her more closely now, his
gaze gleaming with speculation. 'Do
you have any idea how much money is
involved in your grandmother's bequest?'

'No. Do you?'

'Not really, although I could hazard
a pretty good guess. Anyway — ' He

casually brushed the question of the inheritance to one side and Christie didn't feel that she could press him for more detail. It would simply confirm his opinion of her as a gold-digger, if that was indeed what he believed, and he'd given her no reason to doubt it. ' — that aside, I would like to take you out to dinner.' And he gave her what she suspected was a deliberately disarming grin.

Despite her suspicion that he was going out of his way to make himself attractive to her for some unfathomable reason, she discovered herself nodding her assent. She excused her unexpected acquiescence by assuring herself that it was out of curiosity and nothing else. She certainly hadn't been swayed by his unexpected display of charm. After all, what harm could it do? And there was always the chance that she might learn a little more about what made this unusual family tick.

In any case, as she'd already decided, she was well and truly immune to charismatic men. All she had to do to reinforce that resistance was recall one in particular. He'd been every bit as good-looking as Lucas, and he'd betrayed her for weeks on end with someone else. Eventually a close friend had had the compassion to tell her the truth.

Belatedly, she wondered what Toby would have to say about her agreeing to go out with Lucas. He wouldn't like it, that was for sure. He was growing increasingly possessive — mainly, she suspected, because she was here out of his reach. He'd taken to phoning her a couple of times a day, insistently asking, 'Are you okay? I have to say I don't like the sound of this family of yours. I really think I should come down.'

'Toby, I'm fine,' she'd say. 'Stop worrying. It's just for a few more days. I'll soon be back.'

'Good. I can't wait.'

Lucas smiled now in a way that convinced Christie her acceptance of his invitation was only what he had expected. In light of that, she was sorely tempted to retract it and say no. As she'd already decided, he was way too sure of himself. In fact, she wondered whether any woman had ever refused Lucas Grant anything. Maybe she should be the first. But just as she opened her mouth to say she'd changed her mind, he said, 'We'll meet here at eight o'clock this evening.' And with that, he began to walk away.

She surrendered to the inevitable. There was just one thing she needed to know. 'Lucas,' she called after him, 'what sort of place will we be going to? I mean, what should I wear?' She felt naive asking. She was quite sure that the type of woman Lucas usually took out — sophisticated, beautiful, highly intelligent — wouldn't need to ask that question; she would just instinctively know.

However, Lucas didn't look at all surprised or scornful at her request. He simply said, 'Smart casual. Nothing too formal. I don't do formal.' And with that he was gone.

Christie stared after him, still uncertain as to whether she'd done the right thing in agreeing to go out with him. After all, what did she know of him? Other than the fact that he was a successful businessman, if her aunt Alice were to be believed, and the son of her grandfather's god-daughter. He could be a serial rapist for all she knew. But even to her, as distrustful of his motives as she was, that seemed manifestly ridiculous.

In an effort to put things back into perspective, she walked out into the garden. As usual she had her painting things with her, all neatly packed away in a capacious shoulder bag. She'd spotted a hedged garden on one of her strolls and had decided there and then that it would make a perfect subject for a water-colour painting. The high hedges were of neatly trimmed yew; the entrance was through a weather-beaten, lichen-covered gate. Once inside, she'd discovered an enormous variety of ornamental shrubs, as well as large clumps of vibrantly coloured heather and sweet-scented lavender; the garden also contained a central circular pond with a working fountain. But the objects that rendered the scene totally irresistible to her were a pair of antique, she guessed, stone herons positioned so that they seemed to be standing guard on the pond.

As she went through the gateway now, she was sufficiently preoccupied with the question of Lucas and his true motive for asking her out to all but fall over her grandfather in his wheelchair.

'Careful,' he cautioned as he swiv-elled his body to reach backwards and steady her. 'My word, you were miles away then.' His faded blue eyes twinkled up at her. 'Anything I can help with?'

She was pleased to see him. He'd been keeping mainly to his bedroom over the past couple of days. Venetia had told her, 'I think the excitement of your arrival has been a little too much for him.'

'Oh, I'm sorry. I shouldn't have just turned up like I did,' she'd replied, feeling guilty all over again at her unannounced arrival. She should have expected that it might be too much for an elderly couple.

'Nonsense,' Venetia had replied. 'He's thrilled about it. He'll be fine in a day or two. He often gets these periods when he's too tired to do anything.'

Now Christie decided that he had the sweetest smile she'd ever seen. In fact, it reminded her more than anything else had done of her father. 'It's nothing. Well, not really.'

'More painting?' He was eyeing her bag. 'Venetia told me you've been busy.'

'Yes, but that can wait. Would you like to join me in a walk? I could push your chair.'

'That's very kind of you, my dear. There's nothing I'd like more. I don't seem to have had the opportunity to really talk to you yet.' He sighed. 'I get so tired since my stroke twelve months ago. These old bones, this old heart.

Neither of them much use anymore. All worn out.'

Venetia hadn't mentioned a stroke, Christie reflected. Didn't want to worry her, perhaps? 'Don't say that. I've only just found you.' She dropped her bag onto a nearby bench seat and started to push her grandfather's chair along the gravelled pathway that ran around the edge of the enclosed garden. He was very light; too light. No wonder he could be carried up and down the stairs. 'How did you manage to get out here? It's quite a way from the house.' And over quite rough terrain, she mused. It would have taken considerable effort and strength — more than he possessed, she would have thought, to manoeuvre his chair this far unaided.

'Matt pushed me. He's going to return in a while and take me back. Your grandmother thought it was time I had some fresh air.' He turned his head and looked up at her, his expression one of sorrow now. 'I want you to know, Christie, that it was very much against my wishes that Adam was forbidden to return to this house. But, as I'm sure you've noticed by now, your grandmother is a very stubborn woman, and sadly, she has grown only too accustomed to having her own way — in all things. My fault, I know, but I've only ever wanted her to be happy, so I'm afraid I've indulged her a little too much. Shall we go that way?' He pointed to a second gateway on the opposite side to where she'd entered; she hadn't noticed it on her earlier visit. It led out of the garden again. 'I'll show you my pride and joy. Well, it used to be. I have to leave it to Matt nowadays. It's my rose garden.'

'Grandfather, can I ask you something?'

'Of course.'

'Why did my mother leave Uncle Rafe and go off with my father?'

He didn't answer straight away. In fact, he stayed silent for so long that Christie began to wonder whether he'd even heard her. But then suddenly he began to speak, and she realized that he'd only been taking the time to consider her question.

'Well, they weren't happy, that's the first thing. Not even in the beginning. Totally incompatible. But they say love is blind, and I do think she loved him to start with. Rafe is . . . a difficult man, as you've seen for yourself.' He slanted a quizzical glance up at her, but Christie remained silent. It wasn't her place to criticize his son. 'And he didn't treat her very well. He left her alone far too much.' He paused momentarily. 'And Adam was always there. Not surprisingly, nature took its inevitable course.' He shrugged. 'Adam and Rafe were very different to each other . . . '

Again he paused, and Christie felt there was something else he wanted to tell her — maybe a bit more about Rafe and her mother? She regretted now not asking Laura about the causes of the breakdown of her marriage. But of course Laura had been so weak, so ill, that it had taken every ounce of her strength to say as much as she had. Yet simple neglect sounded far too trivial a reason. She and Rafe could have worked a bit harder at saving the relationship, surely? No, there had to be more to it than Rafe being out a lot. Laura had never been a quitter, but that was what she was beginning to sound like. Could it be that Rafe had been unfaithful to Laura? It seemed a reasonable hypothesis, given that he'd spent so much time away from the house.

They'd left the hedged garden behind and entered the sweetly scented rose garden through yet another gateway before her grandfather spoke again. 'Your grandmother didn't see things in that light, however. It was completely unnatural to her, to leave one brother for another. Plus, she hated any family member to be the subject of what she termed vulgar gossip, and here we had three of them involved. Hence, the manner in which she reacted. She came round of course eventually, but Adam wouldn't. Oh well, it was all a long time ago. One thing I would like to know, though — were Adam and Laura happy?'

'Yes; if ever two people were made for each other, they were. My mother wasn't even afraid of dying, because she was convinced she'd see my father again.' Christie's voice broke. Her grandfather reached over his shoulder and patted her hand. 'I can sympathize, but . . . well, Uncle Rafe doesn't like me, does he?'

'Well, I don't know about doesn't like, but you remind him of all that he lost.'

'That wasn't my fault.'

'No, but you have to understand he views you as a threat and, unfortunately, your grandmother has — quite unintentionally, I must stress — fostered that with her intention to change our will. Rafe fully expected to inherit everything. Then, out of the blue, you turn up.'

'I understand that, Grandfather, but

108

that isn't why I came.'

'I know that.'

'And as for the bequest, I really don't want it.'

'Maybe you should try telling your grandmother that.'

'I have. She won't listen.'

'Look.' He turned his head again to look up at her. 'Give Rafe time. He'll come round. He's not really a bad man. And I agree with Venetia. You'll only be getting what's rightfully due to you.'

She wondered about his pronouncement: Rafe was 'not really a bad man'. What did that mean? That in some ways he could be considered so? And where did Lucas figure in all of this? As she'd wondered once before, could he be Rafe's son? They did seem extraordinarily close, closer than Lucas and Victor.

She decided to do a bit of probing. 'Rafe seems very close to Lucas.'

'Yes he is, but we're all fond of Lucas. His mother spent a lot of time here with the two boys, right from when she was quite a small girl. She was my only godchild, so it was devastating when she died. Our one consolation has been Lucas.'

If Lucas was Rafe's son, it didn't sound as if her grandfather knew. But it could explain why Laura had turned to Adam. Had she somehow discovered he already had a child — ?

Victor's next words seemed to confirm her theory. 'And I have to say, Lucas has been remarkably good to Rafe. In return, Rafe looks upon him almost as a son. Whatever is left of Rafe's inheritance upon his death will almost certainly go to Lucas.'

Which meant, Christie mused, that whether or not he was Rafe's son, Lucas had a more than passing interest in what would finally happen to the family money. And that would explain his initial hostility to her arrival. It could also explain why he was so keen to take her out — to try and persuade her to forfeit her inheritance in favour of Rafe.

'He's asked me out tonight,' she said.

'A word of warning then, my dear.' He glanced at her once more, a very shrewd look indeed in his eye. 'Lucas has broken more hearts than I've had hot dinners.'

'My goodness, he must have been busy then,' she quipped. Her grandfather had unwittingly answered another question about Lucas. No woman had ever refused him.

'Just be careful, Christie,' Victor cautioned. 'He won't intend to hurt you, I'm sure, but — '

'Don't worry, Grandfather. It'll take more than Lucas Grant to hurt me.'

5

But that evening, Christie found herself seriously questioning that assertion. Because Lucas was looking dangerously handsome in a tan open-necked shirt and dark cream trousers, the colours emphasizing the leonine look that had so struck her on her arrival.

A shiver of what felt like anticipation went through her as she thanked the Lord that she'd made a quick trip to Plymouth to buy herself a dress; a dress that had a swirly just-above-the-knee skirt, revealing what she considered to be her best features: her shapely legs and ankles. It also sported a neckline that hinted at rather than revealed her deep cleavage. She hadn't at first been inclined to go to so much trouble for someone like Lucas Grant but, as she hadn't brought anything with her to Devon that could be remotely classified as 'smart casual', she'd had no other option.

She couldn't help but notice the interest of the other women in the restaurant in her companion, or their undisguised envy of her. To give Lucas his due, he seemed oblivious to this. But once again, she was glad she'd splurged on a dress that was a bit special.

'So,' he asked as they took their seats, 'how are you liking this part of the country?'

'What I've seen of it — which, admittedly, isn't a great deal so far — I like.'

'How long are you planning to stay?'

'Well, obviously I'd like to stay long enough to get to know my grandparents properly. So ... ' She shrugged. 'Another week or two, maybe.' And that was considerably longer than the few days she'd originally intended. 'It can't be much longer. I need to get back and start sorting out my gallery.'

'I see.' He leant back in his chair,

eyelids lowered, his head slightly tilted back as his hooded gaze travelled lazily over her, tracing each one of her curves as it went.

A quiver passed through her. It was as if his fingers were actually touching her, caressing her. It was all extremely unnerving, and what made the whole experience even worse was that she had no idea what he was thinking. Did he like what he saw, or had he decided she wasn't up to scratch? Was she too thin, or too fat?

Oh God, why did she care what he thought? He was nothing to her. Nonetheless, the result of all of this was that she resorted to her usual practice when subjected to close scrutiny; she started to fidget. She rearranged the cutlery in front of her and straightened her place mat, after which she smoothed any creases from the cloth before twisting her glass round and round by its stem. And all the time, she was acutely aware of his eyes upon her.

Why didn't he look away, or at least

say something? Couldn't he see how uncomfortable he was making her? Or was that his purpose — to keep her on edge; off balance? To ensure she was vulnerable, susceptible to whatever it was he intended? Maybe some sort of demand that she refuse her grand-parents' bequest?

'Am I making you nervous?' he suddenly demanded to know, thereby intensifying her suspicion that he knew exactly what he was doing.

'Why on earth should you think that?' she bit out. Not for anything would she let him know just how successful he'd been, if that had indeed been his intention.

'Well — ' A wry grin twisted his mouth. ' — it could have something to do with the way you've re-laid the table twice over.' His one eyebrow lifted in amusement.

'Have I?' She attempted a light laugh. It didn't quite come off. 'I didn't notice.'

With heartfelt relief, she practically

snatched the menu from the waiter who had just arrived at their table. She briefly scanned it, and then absent-mindedly ordered the lobster bisque to be followed by grilled salmon.

'Very fishy,' Lucas said. He gave his own order and then said, 'Oh, and bring us a bottle of Pinot Grigio, will you? And some water, please.'

'Fishy?' Christie exclaimed. 'What is?'

Was he insinuating that she was up to something? She literally bristled with indignation. Suddenly she wished Saffie were at her side. The two of them together would swiftly see off this — this interloper. Or was she being a bit harsh in labelling him that? He had, after all, been here since he was ten. Which, she supposed, made him more of a member of the family than she was — for all that she was a blood relative, while he . . . well, he was only the son of a god-daughter.

'Your choice of food.'

'Oh, I see.' She didn't really know what she'd thought he'd meant but it hadn't concerned food. Belatedly, she felt foolish.

'Relax, Christie. I won't eat you.'

Hah! Really? His wolfish grin suggested otherwise. Not that she was going to admit to thinking that. He'd most likely tell her she was imagining things. 'I didn't think for a minute that you would.'

'You could have fooled me then.'

'I'm not the least bit nervous.'

'If you say so.' He clearly didn't believe a word of her protest. 'However, your presence at Heron House is making one person in particular very nervous. Rafe. But then, I'm sure you've noticed that for yourself.'

'I wouldn't have described him as nervous. Resentful, maybe. Angry; hostile, even.'

'What did you expect him to be?'

'I hadn't considered it, if you want the truth.'

'You didn't think that your arrival might resurrect some long-buried emotions? Old jealousies? Insecurities? A deep unhappiness? Loneliness, even?'

'As well as a fear of losing what he'd expected to inherit?' she couldn't stop herself from pointedly suggesting, only to immediately think she'd done it again; said too much. Why hadn't she contented herself with simply fidgeting? She held her breath as she waited for the inevitable biting response.

However, all he did was give her a long, level look and say, 'I wasn't at the house at the time, but I do know how deeply he suffered at your mother's desertion of him for his only brother.'

'Well, I'm sure she had her reasons for that,' Christie indignantly said.

'Oh, I'm sure she did, but he was deeply hurt by it all the same. He's never remarried.'

'No?'

'Wouldn't risk being hurt and humiliated like that a second time.'

'Well, maybe he hurt and humiliated my mother first. Have you considered that? I know my mother well enough to be confident that she wouldn't have left

118

without a very good reason.'

Her anger was rising; her breasts heaved. She saw his gaze drop to them and linger, his expression one of unabashed appreciation. Her irritation with him intensified. The lech! How dare he look at her in such a manner? And how dare he sit there and . . . and comment on matters of which he knew very little; judge someone he knew even less of, other than what Rafe had told him? And Rafe would be bound to have been biased about events, told it all from his own perspective. It stood to reason. It was human nature.

He eventually raised his gaze to her face, his eyes smouldering. However, his voice was perfectly level when he spoke, revealing nothing of whatever emotion that heated look had signified.

'Calm down. I'm not criticizing her — or your father, come to that. I'm merely trying to explain why Rafe is reacting as he is to your presence; why he feels as he does. Surely you can understand that?'

'You know how Rafe feels, do you?' she demanded.

'Yes, he's talked to me.'

'Did he tell you what happened between them? Explain why my mother left?'

'Well . . . ' He shrugged.

'Clearly not,' she bit out. Really, she was beginning to sound like an archetypical termagant. The sort of woman she despised, in fact: overbearing, bad-tempered — yet she couldn't stop herself from continuing in the same vein. 'Then I don't think you have any right to pass comment, far less judge anyone concerned.'

He sighed. 'Christie, I'm not judging.'

She heard herself snort contemptuously, only to then wonder why this man was having such an extreme effect on her. She didn't usually behave like this — not even when she was angry.

'I wouldn't presume to do such a thing. I'm merely trying to help you to understand your uncle. To help you

120

become friends. He is the only uncle you have, isn't he?'

'Yes.'

'Well, then — '

At that point, the waiter placed their first courses before them. Lucas ignored his and went on, 'Surely you can understand Rafe's feelings?'

'Yes, in a way,' she grudgingly conceded. 'But I didn't come here for mercenary reasons. I came to meet my grandparents, to get to know them. But mostly because my mother asked me to. Made me promise to, in fact. I'm honouring that promise. I had no notion that there would be any sort of inheritance involved.'

'So why was she suddenly so keen for you to come here? After all, she and Adam had refused to return. What inspired her to make you give such a promise?' There was a disturbing glint in his eye now.

'If you're implying that her motives were financial — ?' she snapped.

'There you go again, turning a

perfectly innocent question into one of accusation. I'm just curious, that's all.'

'Right.' Despite his words, Christie continued to eye him with suspicion. 'She didn't want me to be alone after-after she'd died. I have no siblings; there's just me.' Her voice wobbled.

'I see.'

His expression softened as the amber flecks reappeared within his toffee eyes. Christie felt her pulse begin to race. Did he know how attractive he was? She had a strong suspicion he did only too well, and wasn't above using it for his own ends.

'Well, you've made Victor and Venetia very happy people,' he said. 'It's the next best thing to them having Adam back again. I hope you don't intend to let them down as your parents did.' His voice hardened as his eyes turned steely.

So there it was — a definite threat, the implication being that if she did anything to hurt the two old people, then she'd have him to contend with.

The next morning Christie decided to venture a little further afield than she'd been so far. She felt a quite desperate need to escape the confines of the house and grounds, as extensive as they were — and any possible risk of encountering Lucas. He evidently didn't trust her; had even gone so far as to hint at possible repercussions if she did anything to upset or sadden her grandparents. And that hurt, that he would even think that she would do such a thing.

But what hurt even more was his low opinion of her parents, especially her father. She'd been tempted to contradict him. Point out to him that far from letting anyone down, Adam had merely been protecting Laura, saving the woman he loved from any further unhappiness. However, she'd decided not to bother. He wouldn't believe her, and most likely wouldn't feel any compassion for Adam and Laura and the situation in which they'd found themselves all those years ago. He'd listened to Rafe's version of events and subsequently tried and condemned them both at a stroke. All of which made arguing the rights and wrongs of their actions pretty well futile. She would only be upsetting herself, and she wasn't prepared to do that. He could think whatever he wanted; he was nothing to her and never would be. So his opinions and judgements weren't of any relevance at all.

And yet, after the first few sticky moments, the evening had turned out surprisingly well. Lucas had proved to be an articulate, well-educated man who was running several successful businesses — or, at least, that was how he'd described himself; clearly modesty wasn't one of his qualities — and enjoyed a busy and fulfilled life. That he was immensely fond of the Wakehams was a given fact; that he was extremely protective of Rafe was also self-evident. He'd skilfully drawn Christie into revealing far more about her own life than she'd intended, even winkling facts about Toby out of her. Nothing further had been said of the Wakehams' intention to include Christie in their list of beneficiaries, and he'd made no attempt to persuade her to relinquish her promised inheritance. But then, he could be playing a long game. Win her trust and then move in for the kill.

A chill shivered through her. Maybe that was an unfortunate choice of words. Especially in the wake of the incident that had made her so nervous that first night — finding her door open and hearing something or someone on the landing. But that couldn't have been Lucas, surely? Such an action would invite all manner of accusations, none of them acceptable.

In a bid to banish such disturbing reflections, she decided to take the car and go out somewhere. She was close to Dartmoor, after all. She couldn't return home without exploring some part of it.

She was crossing the hallway to the front door when Rafe hailed her. To say she was surprised would be an under-statement of monumental proportions. Up till then, Rafe had gone to quite extraordinary lengths to avoid her, and when he hadn't been able to manage that, to simply ignore her.

'Where are you off to?' he now asked.

His interest seemed genuine and Christie felt a small thrill of pleasure. Could Lucas have said something to him, thus inspiring him to try and meet her halfway in some sort of uncle-niece relationship? The notion warmed her. Perhaps things were going to turn out all right, after all? Maybe they'd be able to build the sort of relationship that other uncles and nieces enjoyed.

'I'm not sure. I thought I'd take the car and explore the moors. Can you suggest somewhere of interest?' She hefted her bag full of her painting materials onto her shoulder, at the same time trying to make her voice sound as friendly as she could.

'That looks heavy.' Rafe pointed at the bag. 'Not the family silver, I trust?'

Christie stared at him, undecided as to whether he was being serious or not.

'Only joking,' he told her in the next instant. 'After all, you don't need to steal it, do you? Half of it all will eventually be rightfully yours.' His mouth twisted into a sneer of utter contempt.

Christie felt a fury arise the like of which she'd never before experienced, not even with Lucas, as maddening as he could be. How naive she was. How foolish, to hope that things were going to turn out okay; that she and her uncle might just possibly forge a good and loving relationship.

It was then that she asked herself, why shouldn't she accept what her grandparents wanted to give her? Her father would have accepted the bequest, wouldn't he? It was, as both her grandmother and grandfather had pointed out, her due, as their sole grandchild. And it would certainly be welcome, however little it might prove to be. She was going to have to be entirely self-sufficient to support herself. Why not accept a little help from her family? The only family she had now. Tears stung her eyes. Tears she managed, with an iron will, to drive away. She wasn't going to show any signs of weakness in front of this hateful man.

So all she said was a calm, 'Do you know, you're right; it will be. But not just yet, I hope. I'd like the time to get to know both of my grandparents first.'

And with that, she strode smartly through the doorway, heading for her car. The trouble was she was shaking so badly, it was all she could do to place one foot before the other. As it was, she tripped over the doorstep and only just managed to save herself from falling flat on her face.

'I say,' he called after her, 'a word of warning. If you're that clumsy, you'll need to take special care. The moor can be a very dangerous place; much more dangerous than a mere doorstep.' He gave a loud laugh. 'There are lots of bogs, fast-running rivers, nasty things like that. Wouldn't want you to trip into one. You could be badly — even fatally — injured.'

Christie stopped and swivelled to regard him. He was pulling what looked like a hip flask from his coat pocket and lifting it to his lips. He swayed as he took a long swig from it. Why, he was drunk. She'd thought she detected an odour. But, as it was only ten o'clock in the morning, she hadn't even considered it might be alcohol. Was Rafe an alcoholic? Could he have been years ago, too? Was that why Laura had left him — not because of another woman or an illegitimate son?

'Oh, don't worry, I won't.' But she was even more shaken despite her confident-sounding words. Was he hoping she would fall in? Or, even more worryingly, was he threatening her with some sort of physical harm? If he was, then that made two threats that she'd received within twenty-four hours, and both from men she should have felt able to trust.

Despite her deepening disquiet over Rafe and his hostility towards her, Christie managed to work and completed a couple of watercolours as well as several detailed sketches for future paintings. At the end of it all she felt refreshed and more relaxed; her worries, if not forgotten, at least put to one side.

It wasn't until she was nearing the house again that a sense of oppression settled upon her; a sense of apprehension. It was powerful enough to make her wonder if she should think about leaving sooner than the couple of weeks she'd mentioned to Lucas. She could always return in a month or so, when the shock of her sudden arrival had subsided. Yes, maybe that would be best. Rafe would have had time to reflect on things; maybe even begin to accept her presence in his life.

But it wasn't to be.

As she turned the final bend in the

driveway, the first thing she saw was an ambulance. She raced towards it, slamming on her brakes in a swirl of gravel. She leapt from the car and ran over. Her grandmother was standing on the driveway, her face the colour of ancient parchment.

'Grandmother,' Christie gasped, 'what's wrong? What's happened? Are you ill?'

But she could see, even as she voiced the questions, what was wrong. Her grandfather lay inside the vehicle, his eyes closed, his chest barely moving as the paramedics worked on him.

Venetia didn't look at her, her gaze remained fixed upon her husband. 'It's your grandfather.' Every scrap of her matriarchal dignity had deserted her. She looked what she was: a frail old lady, terrified of whatever ordeal it was that lay ahead of her. 'He's had a heart attack.'

6

Christie, her grandmother and her great-aunt followed the ambulance in Christie's car. Alice had run from the house seconds after Christie's arrival and had insisted on accompanying them to the hospital. 'You'll need me, Venetia, in case . . . in case . . . ' The lace handkerchief had appeared as if by magic and she'd mopped her streaming eyes before vigorously blowing her nose.

Venetia, after her initial protest that there was really no need for Alice to go with them, hadn't responded to those final words. In fact, she hadn't seemed to realize what it was Alice was implying. But Christie had known what her great-aunt meant.

In case Victor died.

When they got to the hospital, surprisingly for someone who more often than not appeared frail and slightly scatty, it was Alice who took charge, murmuring encouraging words and holding on tightly to both Venetia's and Christie's hands as they waited anxiously for news. Throughout it all, Venetia sat mute and frozen. She seemed to have aged ten years in as many minutes. As for Christie, she couldn't believe there was a risk that she could lose her grandfather within days of first meeting him. Surely Fate couldn't be that cruel?

But when, finally, the doctor appeared, she knew it could be. Before he even spoke, Christie knew what he was going to tell them.

'I'm very sorry, Mrs Wakeham. There's nothing more we can do.'

They eventually returned to the house to find Rafe, Lucas, Delia and her husband Matt in the hallway. All were ashen-faced with anxiety.

Lucas was the first to speak. 'We were just about to come to the hospital — '

Rafe impatiently cut Lucas off. 'Mother, tell us, please. How is he?'

'Your father died an hour ago,'

Venetia quietly said. She seemed to have regained her customary composure. So much so, that it had been she who'd comforted a weeping Alice on the way home.

'Oh my God,' Rafe cried. His face crumpled and Christie watched helplessly as the tears ran down his face. 'Why wasn't I here? I could have come to the hospital. Been with him.'

An equally grief-stricken Lucas slipped a comforting arm about the older man's shoulders, at the same time looking at Venetia and saying, 'I'm so sorry.' His voice shook with what sounded like deep and genuine emotion.

'Thank you,' Venetia answered, 'but he went peacefully. That, at least, was a blessing. What he would have wanted.'

'I should have been there,' Rafe continued to sob.

'Yes, you should have been. Where were you, Rafe?' Venetia asked, still in that same quiet tone. Although she'd regained her composure, the spirit seemed knocked out of her — not surprisingly, Christie reflected. The man she had so clearly and deeply loved, for all her autocratic manner towards him, had left her. 'I tried ringing you but your phone was turned off.'

In the wake of his mother's questions, Christie noticed that Rafe's tears had completely dried. 'I was with someone; that's why I'd turned . . . ' His words trailed off. He couldn't seem to look at Venetia.

'I see,' was all she said. There was none of the scorn which she usually exhibited towards her elder son. 'Well, don't distress yourself. Now, if you will excuse me, I feel the need for some private time. Alice, perhaps you could come with me?'

'Yes, yes, of course,' Alice readily agreed.

'Grandmother,' Christie began, 'is there anything I can do for you?'

Venetia regarded her with eyes that were shiny with tears. 'Not just at the moment, my dear. Thank you, though. Come, Alice.'

Dinner that night was a low-key affair. Venetia had a tray in her room, and conversation between the remaining four people was practically non-existent. The absence of the old man hung over them all, contributing to an overpowering sense of loss. So much so, that Christie was glad to go to her room once the meal was over. Apart from her immense grief, she felt helpless; superfluous. Maybe now would be a good time to leave, after all. Give the family some space, some privacy, in which to mourn the man they'd all clearly loved so deeply. Much as she'd also come to love her grandfather, she obviously hadn't been as close to him as the rest of them. Her absence from his life till now had seen to that. And she also needed her own quiet time to mourn him; to come to terms with his death so soon after she'd arrived here. She'd come back for his funeral, naturally, and then stay for a while. Her presence, she hoped, would prove a comfort for both her

136

grandmother and her great-aunt.

With all of this in mind, the next morning she sought out her grandmother to tell her what she'd decided. She found her in her bedroom. The old lady was propped up in bed, a breakfast tray upon her lap, the plate of food that sat upon it untouched. She looked extremely frail. Nonetheless, she asked, 'Christie, my dear, how are you?'

'I'm okay. It's you I'm worried about.'

With good reason, she saw as she drew closer. The old lady's cheeks were sunken, her skin grey with exhaustion; her eyes were so colourless they looked transparent, shadows tracing dark grooves beneath them. Her hair, instead of being twisted into its neat bun, hung loose and lank about her shoulders. She looked every day of her eighty years and more besides.

'I'm a little tired, Christie. I didn't sleep much. It's all been a bit of a strain. And now there's the funeral to arrange, and . . . I don't know if I've got the strength.' Her voice shook and she raised a trembling hand to her eyes.

Christie went to her and, removing the tray, sat on the edge of the bed. She took one of the gnarled hands into hers. She didn't say that she'd barely slept either. Her great-aunt's words had echoed in her head all night.

A heron's appearance heralded a death.

That couldn't be true, she'd agonized over and over. It had to be a coincidence, didn't it? Things like that simply didn't happen, not outside of the pages of a book at least.

'Christie . . . ' Her grandmother pressed her fingers tightly. 'You won't go yet, will you? I need you.'

Every vestige of Christie's resolve to leave vanished. She didn't have it in her to refuse this plea; didn't want to, in fact. Her grandmother had said she needed her and that was all that mattered.

'Of course not, not if you don't want me to. But, I will have to go,

Grandmother, eventually.'

'Yes, but not yet. Promise me, please, Christie.' She sounded so anguished that Christie found herself wondering whether she'd sensed that her granddaughter was about to leave.

'I promise.'

★   ★   ★

Christie walked down the stairs some time later, knowing she couldn't leave. As long as her grandmother needed her she'd stay, no matter how long it took. She needed something to absorb her, though, to take her mind off the terrible tragedy of her grandfather's unexpected demise — at least for a brief period. Not painting; that would take her out of the house and she wanted to be near to Venetia, in case her grandmother should have need of her. She'd find a book — not that she had any great hope of being able to concentrate long enough to actually read it. Memories — images — of her grandfather, vivid despite their all-too-brief time together, would intrude, as they'd been doing since the moment he'd been pronounced dead.

'Christie, there you are. Have you seen Venetia this morning?'

It was Lucas. Here was someone else who hadn't slept well, judging by his shadowed eyes.

'Yes, I've just left her.'

'How is she?'

'Grief-stricken.'

'I won't disturb her, but if there's anything I can do . . . ' His stare was a searching one. 'How are you coping?'

She shrugged. 'Oh, you know; I just wish I'd had more time to get to know my grandfather. He was a-a wonderful man.' A small sob stopped her from saying any more.

Lucas's expression softened. 'Well, at least you did meet him; that's something to be thankful for. So what will you do now?'

'Do?'

'Well, you must have to get home.'

'Oh, I see. Yes, but Grandmother needs me, so I've agreed to stay on for a while.'

'Oh — good; good.' He spoke absently, as if he had a great deal on his mind. He showed no emotion at all at her decision to stay at Heron House.

'How's Rafe? He seemed very upset yesterday.'

'He was, but well, he's gone out, so . . . ' He, too, shrugged.

'Does he have a drink problem?' She blurted the question out. She simply couldn't help herself, she had to ask. It might not seem the right time, but . . .

Lucas's eyes darkened until they were the colour of treacle. There was no sign of the amber glints. 'That's his own affair, surely.'

'Well, yes, but he looked a little strange yesterday morning when I saw him. He was drinking straight from a hip flask and-and he said some peculiar things.'

'What sort of things?'

'Things like I should be careful out on the moor. You know, watch out for

141

bogs, fast-running rivers . . . ' Her words trailed off. Put like that, it did sound pretty harmless. Had she imagined the implied threat? She hadn't thought so at the time.

'He was simply warning you, wouldn't you say?'

'Yes, yes, I-I'm sure you're right. Well, I'll maybe see you later.'

'Yes.'

She felt Lucas's gaze following her as she carried on towards the library. She glanced back just the once; he hadn't moved and his expression was hooded and totally unreadable.

★   ★   ★

Three days later, and completely out of the blue, Toby arrived. Christie couldn't believe how pleased she was see him. Suddenly her irritation at his growing possessiveness over her fled. He was someone she could trust — and, of late, she'd increasingly felt the need for that.

She'd been spending a large part of

her time with Venetia. She seemed to be the only person that the old lady would tolerate with her. When Christie had suggested that either Rafe or Alice would probably like to see her, her sole response had been, 'Tell me about your father. I want to hear about everything that happened after he left here. Everything.'

Christie decided that hearing about Adam must be providing some degree of solace for her grandmother in the wake of losing her husband. So she talked until her throat ached, dredging up own memories of her father as well as anecdotes which her mother had told her over the years and which she'd believed she'd long forgotten about. Venetia thirstily drank it all in. Her questions were endless, some of which Christie could answer, some she couldn't. Alice put her head around the door a couple of times, as did Rafe, but they were both given short shrift. At one point she heard Venetia mutter, 'I don't know why I've put up with it all these years.' Christie couldn't help but wonder, put up with what? Having Alice living there? But Alice did a lot for her sister, and she must be a source of comfort now — ?

But it was Venetia's dismissal of Rafe that worried Christie the most. The look of venom that had crossed his face had been directed solely at Christie. Surely Venetia could see that such treatment of her remaining son would only make an already fraught situation even worse? He'd view Christie more and more as the sole obstacle standing in his way of what she presumed, from his behaviour towards her, would be a pretty substantial inheritance.

And, in the light of what she'd interpreted as his barely veiled threats, who knew what he'd do about that?

Only Lucas had been well received and, by the gleam that would appear in Venetia's eye when the three of them were together, Christie suspected that her grandmother hadn't abandoned her match-making despite her ongoing grief

144

for her husband.

So when Toby arrived, it seemed only natural for Christie to fall into his arms. 'Tobes! What a wonderful surprise.'

'Well, well,' he laughed, 'if I'd known what a rapturous welcome I'd be given I'd have come sooner.'

She'd rung and told him about her grandfather's sudden death. He'd sounded concerned for her, deeply, but he'd made no mention of a visit.

'You sounded so down, and I didn't want to put anyone to any trouble at this time, which if I'd warned you I most probably would have — so I just packed a bag, booked a room at the hotel down the road, and told the powers that be at work that there was a family emergency. Well, you are almost family,' he responded to Christie's wry glance. 'And so, here I am. I've missed you, Christie.' And with that, he proceeded to kiss her with the sort of forceful determination she recalled from their last meeting when she'd told him where she was going.

Not wishing to fuel whatever hopes he was entertaining about their future together — not while she was so uncertain herself of what it was she wanted, she was about to pull free when he released her quickly and of his own accord. He was staring beyond her. Christie swivelled her head to see Lucas descending the stairs.

'Well.' Lucas's expression was unfathomable, as it so often was. Christie had never known anyone so maddeningly adept at concealing their thoughts and emotions. 'Aren't you going to introduce me, Christie?'

'Of course,' she responded. 'Toby, this is Lucas; Lucas, Toby.'

'Aah yes, Toby,' Lucas drawled. 'I believe Christie mentioned you the other evening while we were out having dinner. I didn't realize we were about to be favoured with a visit.' He looked enquiringly at Toby.

Toby, for his part, was startled by all of this and his subsequent glance at Christie was an uncertain one. This

146

almost instantly turned to surprise as he asked, 'Um — out having dinner?'

His surprise wasn't misplaced. Christie hadn't been exactly complimentary about Lucas during their many phone conversations.

'Yes,' Christie lamely agreed. 'We — '

'I invited Christie out,' Lucas interrupted. 'I thought we should become, uh, better acquainted. After all, I am a *very* close friend of the family.'

Christie frowned. It almost sounded as if Lucas was being deliberately provocative. But if he was, why?

'Lucas has his own apartment here.'

'I see,' Toby murmured, although he quite evidently didn't. He swung back to Christie. 'Darling.' He smiled at her intimately, putting an arm around her and pulling her to his side.

Christie gazed at him, bemused. Toby had never, ever called her darling. It wasn't his style at all. And this demonstration of . . . well, possessive intimacy, was totally out of character. What was going on here between these

147

two? A bit of macho rivalry? A combined surge of testosterone?

'I didn't wish to put anyone to any trouble, so I've booked a room at a small hotel nearby.'

'Splendid,' cut in Lucas. 'Any friend of Christie's is welcome. I'm sure Venetia would endorse that. Look, why don't you invite Toby to dinner tonight, Christie? I'm sure your grandmother will wish to meet him, not least to vet him as a suitable companion for her only granddaughter.' He glanced again at Toby. 'Did Christie tell you that her grandfather has only recently died? As you can imagine, it's been a particularly sad time for us all. We haven't really seen anyone outside of the immediate family.'

'Yes, Christie rang me. That's the main reason I came. She sounded so distressed.' Toby was beginning to look edgy; ill at ease. 'Look, if it's inconvenient I'll go again. I wouldn't want to intrude.'

Lucas stayed silent, although there

was a strange expression upon his face. Christie found herself wondering whether he could be trying to drive Toby away by making him feel unwelcome; an intruder. But why would he do that? To make Toby jealous? Again, she asked herself why. He'd displayed no real interest in her other than for the odd appraising glance. Although she recalled the manner in which his hooded gaze had roamed over her the other evening, and the way her body had quivered in response.

'No, Toby, there's no need for that,' Christie hastily interrupted. 'You've only just arrived; you can't simply turn around and go again. Can he, Lucas?'

Her attempt to shame Lucas into extending the hand of welcome must have worked, because he immediately said, 'Of course not. As a friend of Christie's, you're most welcome, Toby. And a new arrival, I'm sure, will divert us all at dinner. Just what we need — especially Venetia. She'll have great fun finding out all about you.'

Christie regarded his sudden change

of tack with suspicion. What was he up to?

★   ★   ★

Christie had been to Venetia's bedroom to tell her about Toby's arrival and to warn her of his presence at dinner that evening. Her grandmother hadn't looked at all pleased about that, Christie suspected because she viewed him as some sort of threat to her hopes of an eventual union between Christie and Lucas.

'You haven't mentioned him previously, Christie,' she'd said.

'Well, I didn't think it was important, Grandmother. I mean, it's not as if we're engaged or anything.' Nor likely to be, she almost added, but stopped herself just in time. She wouldn't put it past her grandmother to repeat that to Toby, and she wanted to tell Toby herself that his hopes were in vain; that was the least she owed him.

'Hmmm.' Venetia had eyed her. 'Well, if we've got a guest I'd better change

150

my clothes.' She was at present wearing a skirt and blouse that had definitely seen better days. Venetia's grief seemed to have imbued her with an uncharacteristic disregard for how she looked. Up till now, she'd invariably been as neat as a pin, wherever she'd been or whatever she'd been doing.

'Toby won't expect anything grand, Grandmother.'

'He'll get whatever I decide to wear,' her grandmother sharply retaliated.

Christie departed for her room. Knowing her grandmother, as she'd come to, she'd dress up for a guest. It would be her notion of courtesy. Accordingly, Christie donned the dress she'd bought to go out with Lucas.

However, her grandmother surprised her. She'd made less effort than usual. In fact, her attire could best be described as casual: a light sweater and a skirt. They were a degree smarter than the ones she'd had on earlier, but even so, the outfit had the look of a charity shop purchase about it. Clearly she'd decided to take Christie's words literally. As a result Christie, in stark contrast to her first evening there, felt inappropriately overdressed. So it didn't help that when Toby arrived, he was also smartly dressed. However, Venetia didn't seem to notice and immediately began to ply him with questions.

The rest of them could only sit by and listen — Lucas, she saw, with a maddeningly provocative smile.

Christie stared at him, not bothering to hide her irritation. He'd known this would happen. That was what he'd meant by a diversion, and why he'd suggested Christie invite Toby — not to welcome him as a friend of Christie's, but to intensify Toby's feeling of being in the wrong place at the wrong time. And to deliberately subject him to her grandmother's grilling. Huh! Grilling, she mused; it was more like an inquisition. She scowled at him at one point, to no avail. Lucas simply met her gaze with his usual composure and even had the nerve to raise his glass to her.

'Why didn't you tell us you had a special friend, Christie?' had been Venetia's opening salvo.

Christie watched as Toby, rather unsuccessfully it had to be said, struggled to hide his smile. He'd probably never heard himself described as someone's 'special friend' before.

Without allowing Christie time to answer, her grandmother had gone on. 'So what precisely do you do, um, Toby?' Venetia's expression said it all as she spoke his name. She evidently considered it only appropriate for the rather ugly jugs that sat upon the dresser in the kitchen.

Christie quite clearly heard Lucas's soft snort of amusement at all of this. Venetia heard it too. She looked at him and frowned. 'Did you say something, Lucas?'

'No, just clearing my throat, Venetia.'

'Humph!' She turned back to Toby, obviously expecting an answer to her question.

'I work for the engineering firm that

Christie used to be with.'

Lucas drawled, 'Much future there? Obviously Christie didn't think so, as she left.'

Toby met Lucas's sceptical gaze with confidence. 'Well, that's where I disagree with Christie. If I didn't see a future there, I wouldn't be staying.'

A surge of pride in him arose within Christie. He was more than holding his own against these people who seemed determined to put him down; to relegate him to the realms of the insignificant. However, so vexed was she by Lucas's patronizing manner that Christie couldn't help snapping, 'Toby is destined for big things, Lucas; especially now that Bristow's have taken Pringle's over. You have heard of Bristow's, I presume? They're the largest — '

'Yes, I know. I also know the owner rather well. Jeremy Bristow. We quite often have a game of golf together. He has a country house not far from here; spends most of his weekends there. He told me he'd taken over Pringle's. I didn't realize that that's who you'd worked for, Christie. He intends to expand the business globally. Plenty of prospects there, I'd have said. Maybe you should have stayed.' His gaze was a challenging one.

She didn't respond. She wouldn't give him the satisfaction of rising to his gibe.

'I tried working for an engineering firm once,' Rafe remarked. 'Couldn't get on with it at all. Pretty swiftly gave it up, I can tell you.'

'Yes, well,' Venetia interrupted, 'you've tried many things, haven't you, Rafe? Couldn't seem to get on with any of them, as I recall.' Her tone as she mimicked his words was once again scornful, her fleeting compassion for his distress over his father's death obviously put on the back burner. 'What is it they say? Jack of all trades, master of none.'

'That's very unfair, Venetia,' Alice protested — as she invariably did.

'Maybe, Alice, but true nonetheless. What's Rafe ever done that's been worthwhile? That's actually earned him any money?'

Christie stole a glance at Toby. Whatever must he be making of all this? Firstly he'd been subjected to what could only be described as an inquisition; now the family were bickering amongst themselves, seemingly oblivious to the presence of a guest. Toby's face, however, gave nothing away, although his eyes did begin to dart nervously from one person to another, probably trying to anticipate what would come next. If he was, he wasn't left wondering for long.

Rafe's complexion, florid at the best of times, turned puce. He leapt to his feet, throwing his napkin down onto the table, where it landed in the remains of his dinner, splashing gravy all over the pristine tablecloth. 'That is so typical of you, Mother. Always knocking me, putting me down. Nothing I ever do is good enough.'

'But don't you see? That's the trouble, Rafe.' Venetia's tone now was that of someone conducting a perfectly reasonable conversation. 'You don't do anything. Except empty the whisky bottle, of course, and spend money. You're an expert at both of those. Do you think they could be called occupations?' she asked the diners collectively.

'Venetia!' Alice burst out. She gazed beseechingly at Lucas. 'Lucas? Say something.'

'Venetia,' Lucas began. Despite the glitter of anger behind his eyes, he spoke gently. He was clearly at pains not to upset the old woman so soon after her husband's death. 'That's needlessly cruel of you.'

But his intervention came too late. Rafe had already stormed from the room, slamming the door behind him. The next sound to be heard was the deep-throated revving of a car engine. Rafe had gone out.

'Really, Venetia.' Alice, too, got to her feet. 'You're too bad. What has Rafe ever done to you?'

'Don't ask stupid questions, Alice.

You know perfectly well what Rafe has done to me. He's sponged off me all of his life. Maybe if you stopped taking his side and mollycoddling him, he'd turn into the man he should have been.'

'Well, what did you expect? That I'd castigate him too? I'm hardly likely to do that, am I?' And with that oblique statement she, too, left the room.

'I do think you were a bit hard on Rafe, Venetia.' Lucas glanced at Christie before sweeping his gaze to Toby. 'And whatever must our guests be thinking?'

Guests! Christie reflected, feeling understandably indignant as well as more than a little hurt. She was hardly a guest. In fact, she had more right to be there than he did. She was, after all, Venetia's granddaughter, whereas what was he? Merely the son of a god-daughter. Or was she just being petty now?

'I apologize if I've embarrassed anyone.' Every trace of colour had drained from Venetia's face. 'I-I really don't know what came over me. It was inappropriate at such a time.' She passed a shaky hand across her eyes. She looked deflated; intensely vulnerable.

Christie stumbled to her feet, as did Lucas. 'Grandmother,' Christie cried, 'are you all right?'

'I'm fine; just very, very tired. Toby, it was a pleasure to meet you, but you'll all have to excuse me now. I need some time alone. I think I'll go to my room. Lucas, will you assist me?'

'Christie — ' Venetia looked back just once as Lucas steered her from the room. ' — take Toby into the small sitting room. Delia will bring you coffee. Once again, forgive me.'

7

'Phew,' said Toby once they were seated side-by-side on a settee in the sitting room, 'is dinner always that eventful?'

'We-ell, not usually.'

She had no intention of revealing that such arguments seemed to take place with disturbing frequency; it would sound dangerously like criticism of her newfound family. But it was so unlike her grandmother to apologize for anything that Christie's anxiety about her state of mind in the aftermath of her husband's death intensified.

'Your grandmother was a bit hard on your uncle. Your aunt seemed very protective of him, though.'

'Yes, she is. She's very fond of him. But then, he is her only nephew.'

'Look, don't take this the wrong way,' Toby went on, 'but I don't think I can go through another evening like this one has been. Sorry, is that a bit blunt?'

'No, it's okay. I understand. It was a bit tense, wasn't it?'

Toby let out a shout of laughter. 'Now there's an understatement if ever I heard one. But, look — why don't we go out, just the two of us, tomorrow? We could drive somewhere for the day, then come back to Plymouth, maybe get dinner somewhere. I can't go back without venturing onto Dartmoor.'

'Oh Toby, I'd love that, and I'm sure Grandmother won't mind.'

But would she? She seemed to want Christie to stay nearby. And apart from that, Christie was pretty sure that Venetia hadn't welcomed Toby's arrival; far from it, in fact. He would, as a 'special friend' of Christie's, qualify as a major obstacle in the way of her plans for Lucas and Christie's future together.

However, Toby knew nothing of this and so beamed his delight at her. He slipped an arm around her shoulders. 'I know it hasn't been long, but I've missed you terribly.'

'Yes, you said.' Christie instinctively stiffened the second Toby touched her. Was he going to kiss her? All of a sudden, she knew that she didn't want him to. Toby wasn't the one for her. She was immensely fond of him and always would be, but she knew now it wasn't the kind of love you'd feel for a prospective husband. It was the kind of love you'd feel for a close friend or a brother, and their kisses had reflected that. They'd been almost platonic, with none of the passion that lovers felt — until the last couple of times, that was.

She gnawed on her bottom lip. She'd been so stupid, welcoming him with such impetuous warmth. He'd read far more into that than she'd intended. But the truth was, she'd been so pleased to see his familiar face after the tensions of the past few days that she'd kissed him without giving any consideration to the consequences. And she was going to have to pay for that heedlessness now. Anyway, apart from her not welcoming his lovemaking, supposing someone should come in? Lucas, for instance?

'Um, Toby . . . ' She pulled away from him.

'Okay, okay, you don't need to say it. Neither the time nor the place, eh?' His eyes gleamed at her, full of unmistakable promise.

Christie sighed. He was thinking of the next day when they'd be alone together. That was why he'd suggested they go out. Not for the reasons he'd stated. He wanted to make love to her, and the truth was she couldn't let him; didn't want to let him.

She should tell him that, right now, that there was no future for them as a couple. It was the only thing to do; the fair thing to do. 'Toby — '

But that was as far as she got, because he leapt to his feet and, obviously misunderstanding her intention, said, 'I know, time to leave. I'll give the coffee a miss if you don't mind. It's been a long day, and the rather comfortable-looking bed in my hotel room is beckoning. So, I'll let you have an early night and I'll see you in the morning. Okay?'

'Yes, all right.' She didn't have the heart or will to dampen the enthusiasm written all over his face, not just at the moment. She'd tell him before he left again. All she had to do tomorrow was somehow prevent him from trying to make love to her. The trouble was, she suspected that that might not be the easiest thing in the world to do. He'd been very forceful when he'd kissed her earlier; uncharacteristically forceful.

'I'll see you out,' she said.

He eyed her. 'Are you sure you're okay? You look a bit . . . well, flat, I suppose. Depressed.'

'Well, recent events haven't had me jumping for joy, exactly, Toby.'

How could he have forgotten her grandfather's death so easily? What did he expect? That she'd be the same as she'd always been? For heaven's sake, she'd lost her mother and her grandfather both in a space of a couple of

164

months. Toby was usually more sensitive than this to the emotions of others.

'Of course. Sorry, love.' He grinned ruefully. 'That was tactless of me. I should have thought. You barely had time to get to know your grandfather. That must be hard to deal with.' They'd reached the front door by this time and Toby pulled it open. 'Say my goodnights, will you? And my thanks for dinner.' He hesitated, as if reluctant to leave. 'Ten o'clock all right to pick you up tomorrow?'

She nodded. She felt exhausted; it had been a long day for her, too, and the evening had been a particularly stressful one. 'Yes, that's fine. Goodnight, Tobes.' The nickname sprang easily to her lips; too easily. For the second time, she gnawed at her bottom lip as she saw Toby register the small intimacy. He was bound to take that as encouragement.

He did. He instantly bent his head to hers. 'Night, love.'

He was going to kiss her. Christie did

the only thing she could: she turned her head so that his lips landed rather clumsily upon her cheek rather than her mouth. He registered that too, but apart from a slight darkening of his eyes, he didn't respond to the unmistakable rebuff. Nonetheless, she sensed his disappointment as well as his perplexity.

'I'll see you tomorrow,' she said.

Christie closed the door behind him and with a sigh, leant back against it. It was then that she heard the unmistakable sounds of someone moving around upstairs. She glanced up but there was no light on, and no one to be seen. Memories of the first night she'd spent here resurfaced. She'd never discovered who that had been out on the landing — if indeed it had actually been someone and not just her imagination working overtime. She moved away from the door and began to slowly climb the stairs.

'Oh, I was just bringing you some coffee, Miss Wakeham; you and your friend.'

It was Delia bearing a tray with a cafetiere and two cups upon it. 'Would you like to take it up with you?'

Heavens, Christie thought, did Delia assume Toby was in her room waiting for her? She'd better explain. She didn't want any sort of misconception getting back to her grandmother. The old lady would be horrified, she was sure. She suspected that Venetia had very strict morals, especially where her only granddaughter was concerned. 'Yes, that would be nice. Um — sorry, Toby was tired and decided to go back to his hotel. The journey down from the Midlands, you know . . . '

'You don't have to explain to me, Miss Wakeham.' She paused. 'Will we be seeing him again?'

'I'm not sure. He's taking me out for the day tomorrow and then we'll probably have dinner somewhere in Plymouth.' Something had just occurred to her. 'Can you recommend a good restaurant, Delia?'

'I surely can.' Delia proceeded to

issue a stream of directions to a place that she and Matt went to now and again on their evenings off. 'We've always had a lovely meal there. It's good without being too pricey. Not that I'm saying the young man couldn't afford . . . ' Her words tailed off in embarrassment.

Christie smiled. 'I'm sure you're not, but it's always good to find somewhere nice without paying the earth. Toby will appreciate that, as will I.'

'Well, they only use locally caught fish and home-produced meat. They even grow their own vegetables for salads, I believe.'

Eventually Christie managed to make her escape — she was discovering that Delia could be quite a chatterbox once she got going — and, carrying the tray with just one cup on it now, continued on up the stairs. As she did so, she heard the sounds of someone on the landing once again. When she got there, however, just like that first night, whoever it had been had gone.

* * *

That night her sleep was disturbed for the second time by a noise outside of her room. It sounded like someone scratching on the carpet. It couldn't be Delia. She wouldn't be cleaning at this time of night, would she? Suddenly there was a bang on the door; it didn't sound like a hand. It was more as if someone had fallen against it.

Thoroughly alarmed now, she switched on the bedside lamp and leapt out of bed to run to the door. Could it be her grandmother out there? Had there been some sort of accident? She yanked the door open, too anxious to be cautious and looked out.

'Grandmother?'

She could see no one. A growl sounded. She glanced down. Rafe's dog was there, mere inches away, looking up at her, his teeth bared in a ferocious snarl, clearly poised to launch himself at her.

She acted out of pure instinct then

and slammed the door closed before the animal could move. The wretched thing had been going to attack her. She could still hear it, scratching and growling.

'Samson,' she heard Rafe's voice calling, 'here. Now.'

My God, did he roam the house unsupervised at night? Had it been Samson who'd pushed the door open that first night? The mere notion horrified her. He could have been on the point of entering her room to attack her where she lay in bed.

No, be sensible, she cautioned herself. She'd thought she'd seen someone or something, a movement of some sort, and it hadn't looked like a dog; it had been something much larger, like a person. Could it have been Rafe looking for Samson? Had he been expecting the animal to be in her room? Had he been the one to open her door and look in, expecting to see her lying wounded with Samson standing over her?

Shivering at the mere notion of that, she went back to bed. She could be in danger. But whether from Samson or his owner, she couldn't have said. Or was she overreacting — perceiving danger where there was none? She didn't know and that made it all the more disturbing.

She didn't think she would, but she did eventually sleep, and awoke to a morning that held the promise of warmth and sun to come. In the light of day her fears of the night before seemed exaggerated and irrational. Yet, the fact was that Samson had been outside her door trying to get in. But maybe she'd imagined the menace emanating from him? Maybe he'd been growling at her simply because she was a stranger? She certainly hoped so, because otherwise she couldn't see how she could stay there.

Hoping to distract herself from what had happened, she leant out of the bedroom window. The scent of roses wafting towards her on the breeze had her recalling her walk in the garden with her grandfather. She sighed. She'd give anything, absolutely anything, to have him back; to have the opportunity to really get to know him. To be able to talk to him, confide her deepening misgivings and have him reassure her. Why oh why hadn't she been told of him earlier? She could have visited during school holidays. But at least her grandmother was still here, so she had that to be thankful for.

She dressed in a pair of lightweight cropped trousers and a strappy top for her and Toby's day out. She threw a sweater over her arm just in case it should cool off later on.

She'd eaten and was waiting outside on the driveway by ten o'clock precisely. There'd been no sign of anyone else at breakfast. Delia had informed her that both Venetia and Alice had had trays taken to their rooms, and where Rafe was she had no idea. As for Lucas — well, he had businesses to run, so she hadn't expected to see him anyway. In any case, she suspected he made a habit of eating the first meal of the day in his apartment in privacy. She'd rarely seen him that early. Of course, she supposed he could still be in bed, but something — her intuition — told her that Lucas wasn't a shirker.

'Will you tell Grandmother that I've gone out for the day?' Christie had asked the housekeeper. 'My mobile phone will be on so if she should want me, here's the number.' She handed Delia one of the cards she'd had printed. 'I'll come straight back.'

'Of course I'll tell her. But from what she said earlier, when I took her breakfast up, I think she's planning a quiet day. Don't you worry; I'll keep an eye on her.'

It was a quarter past the hour before Toby arrived. He pulled to a halt in a swirl of gravel and leapt from the car.

'Sorry, sorry. Overslept.' He grinned at her and then said 'Hi' before depositing a light kiss on her cheek. He made no attempt to turn the caress into anything more than what it was: a friendly greeting.

Christie breathed a soft sigh of relief. Maybe her coolness of the evening before had given him a clue about her emotions — or lack of them, rather? She hoped so. She didn't want her rejection of him and his love to come as too big a shock. The last thing she wanted was to lose Toby as a friend. Sadly, she suspected that that would be the inevitable outcome.

'So!' He rubbed his hands together, his enthusiasm for the day ahead plain to see. Again, Christie felt a reluctance to burst his bubble of happiness and hope. Maybe she should leave things as they were until she returned home. Why spoil her and Toby's brief time down here together? But she knew she couldn't do that — couldn't let him go on hoping, planning. It would be cruel. It would also give him expectations that she had no intention of fulfilling. She had to tell him and it had to be before he left.

'Where shall we go? Any ideas?'

Christie had found a map of the local area, including nearby Dartmoor, and had gone to the lengths of working out a route. She spread the map across the bonnet of Toby's car and traced with a finger the road they would take. It crossed great swathes of moorland, most of which she herself hadn't seen either.

'Looks great!' he enthused. She told him then of the restaurant that Delia had recommended. 'Good, good. We'll do that. So, ready?' Good humour radiated from him, bestowing an air of almost rakishness.

He wasn't as handsome as Lucas but he was attractive in a warm and unassuming way, with his chestnut-coloured hair and eyes the exact shade of malt whisky. He also possessed a good bone structure with prominently high cheekbones, a long, straight nose and a full mouth that was prone to smiling.

Christie felt a piercing of anguish at

the notion that later that day that smile would undoubtedly vanish and she might never see it again. She'd miss it; miss him. So why couldn't she return his feelings?

However, that was for later. Firmly, she shook herself free of the disturbing prospect of Toby's distress and climbed into the passenger seat of his car.

The day turned out to be an idyllic one, the scenery breathtakingly beautiful. They ventured into remote areas that Christie would never have ventured into alone. Delia had done them proud and prepared a packed lunch fit for a king — and queen. They ate it, sitting companionably on the grassy bank of a wide, fast running river. At one point, a kingfisher flew in front of them, skimming the water with its gloriously iridescent wings.

'Oh' Christie gasped, 'did you see that, Tobes?'

Then there were the ponies that roamed freely, although she'd heard that there weren't as many as there used to be. She wished she'd brought her sketchpad, or at the very least her camera. There was so much here she'd love to paint. Not least the craggy tors that freckled the landscape and that Dartmoor was so famous for.

Eventually, sated with food and a glass of wine each, as well as the sheer loveliness of their surroundings, they strolled back to the car and continued their wandering, stopping frequently to get out and walk to view something which had caught their attention.

Finally, and with a great deal of regret, they left the moorland behind and headed for Plymouth and the restaurant where they intended to dine. The sun was beginning its lazy descent, gently bathing everything in gold as it did so. To her relief, Toby hadn't made any attempt to make love to her. Maybe he'd realized it would be futile; maybe he'd accepted there was no future for them as a couple. She hoped so. It would hurt her as much as him to end things between them.

The restaurant, when they reached it, was small — more of a bistro, with only a dozen or so tables, each one covered with a crimson cloth laid over a larger white one upon which sat silver cutlery, genuine crystal glasses and a small vase of sweetly scented flowers. There was also a chunky candle, already lit and glowing. It was cosy and intimate, and the smells that emanated from the kitchen almost guaranteed a delicious meal. They also sharpened the pangs of hunger in Christie that had been making themselves felt for the past hour or so. The journey back to Plymouth had taken longer than she'd anticipated, mainly because they'd got lost at one point, and she'd begun to worry that the bistro would have stopped serving food.

But there was no sign of that. The maître d' made them feel very welcome, and when some other people walked in after them, she knew her fears had been groundless. There was no sense of hurry or rush.

They were shown to a table in front of the window that looked out onto a busy main road. Cars and people swept by in an endless procession, quite a few pedestrians pausing to read the menu in the window. All of the remaining tables bar one were swiftly filled. The empty one sported a 'reserved' sign. Someone had clearly planned in advance, unlike her and Toby.

The food, as Delia — and the aromas drifting from the kitchen — had promised, was utterly delicious. They both relaxed and gave themselves up to the sheer pleasure of consuming it.

That was until Lucas Grant walked in.

He was accompanied by the loveliest woman Christie had ever seen. Not that she was at all surprised by that. She couldn't, for the life of her, see Lucas Grant escorting an ugly female. Not his style at all. Which was why she'd been so astonished when he'd asked her out. Not that she was ugly — at least, she hoped she wasn't. But this woman, so glamorous she would be at home on a West End stage or even in films, was exactly what she would have expected, and cast her well and truly into the shade.

No, what she was surprised by was the fact that he should turn up on the very same evening that she and Toby were there. Coincidence, she suddenly wondered, or something a bit more contrived? Could he have known they'd be here?

'What's he doing here?' Toby quietly asked. 'Did you tell him we were coming?' His tone now was one of accusation, as was his expression.

'No,' she exclaimed, 'of course I didn't. I haven't even seen him — uh-oh, he's spotted us; he's coming over,' she then hissed. She plastered what she hoped was an unconcerned smile onto her face. 'Lucas,' she said as he got nearer, 'fancy seeing you.'

He didn't immediately respond, other than to nod at her and then Toby. Christie stared up at him as he swept his glance back to her and held her gaze. Christie's breath halted in her throat. Something in his expression told her that her suspicion was the correct one; he'd known they'd be here. Which meant it must have been him on the landing the evening before. He'd overheard her and Delia talking. But why on earth would he follow them here?

'It's one of my favourite places,' he said, his expression so impassive that she found herself wondering whether she'd imagined that previous look. 'I'm a regular. Oh, let me introduce Summer.'

Christie was forced to hurriedly swallow a giggle of amusement. Summer? Although why she was surprised, she couldn't have said. Would any woman this lovely be a common or garden Jane or Anne? Of course not. Summer was perfect, she decided with more than a touch of cynicism.

'Summer — ' Lucas placed an arm around Summer's waist, pulling her forward as well as closer to him. ' — this is Christie and, uh, Toby, a good friend of Christie's. Christie is Mrs Wakeham's granddaughter.'

Summer smiled vaguely in Christie's direction. She managed it without actually looking at Christie, and also managed to do no more than brush the very tips of Christie's outstretched fingers before instantly withdrawing her perfectly manicured hand. It was as if she wished Christie to know that she didn't mix with ordinary mortals, and certainly didn't exchange touches with them.

Christie couldn't help herself: she raised an eyebrow and slanted a glance at Toby. She could see that Toby, too, was struggling to contain his mirth. It induced a hastily smothered giggle on Christie's part. As for Lucas, she didn't dare look at him; she wasn't at all sure that he wouldn't be able to read her thoughts. He'd been remarkably perceptive on at least a couple of occasions, but really — what on earth was he doing with this vacuous-looking woman? In fact, Christie would be amazed if she'd ever had a constructive thought or opinion about anything. Or was she being needlessly cruel now?

Feeling more than a little guilty at her own bitchiness, Christie said a warm 'Nice to meet you, Summer.' She looked at Lucas then — she couldn't help it; his gaze drew her. His eyes were gleaming as he watched her. Of course, he'd seen straight through her. She should have expected that.

However, he very clearly didn't give a damn what she or anyone else thought of his companion. But still — Christie, if asked, would have said that he would go for a woman of intelligence, one with a high IQ; one who would be his intellectual equal. One with whom he could enjoy enlightened conversation, discuss current events with, talk business with, maybe. Could this woman even speak? It would appear not. Summer was gazing round the room, her expression empty; bored, even.

'Enjoying the food?' Lucas eventually asked — well, drawled, really.

'Yes, it's excellent.' Toby must have

decided it was time he said something, especially in the light of Christie's total silence.

'And have you enjoyed your day?'

So, he did know what they'd been doing. In which case, the sounds she'd heard on the landing the evening before had definitely been him; there was no other explanation. Either that, or Delia had mentioned Christie and Toby's plans. Somehow she doubted that the housekeeper would have done that. But why would he turn up here? To demonstrate that he had a glamorous girlfriend? Why on earth would he think she'd care?

'Yes.' Both she and Toby spoke at the same time.

A smile quirked Lucas's lips. 'Such enthusiasm,' he drawled. 'How sweet.'

Christie instantly felt like a girl again, a girl who had been reprimanded for being over-eager. 'Well, why not?' she waspishly responded. 'Dartmoor is a very beautiful place.'

'Quite. Well, nice to see you both. I'll let you get on with your food. Summer,' he went on, moving his arm so that he could now cup her elbow with his hand, 'let's find our table. It must be that one over there.'

'One would assume so,' Christie softly murmured, 'as it's the only table free.'

Lucas didn't respond, other than to slant a glance down at Christie and give another provocative smile. Christie pretended to ignore him. However, her lips tightened as she watched the pair go to their table, Summer still not having uttered a single word.

'Good grief!' Toby whispered. 'Talkative, wasn't she? What on earth does he see in her — other than the obvious, of course?' he concluded.

It didn't help that Christie had had the very same thought. Even so, she would have thought Lucas would have been a bit more discriminating in his choice of girlfriend. After all, beauty wasn't everything.

She tried very hard after that to disregard the couple on the other side of the room and devote herself to finishing off the rest of her meal. It proved almost impossible, though, and to her vexation she found her glance straying time and again to Lucas and his companion.

Lucas, aside from one instance when he seemed to sense Christie's gaze upon him and returned it with a barely visible smile and a raised glass, kept his attention firmly fixed upon his lovely girlfriend. Not surprisingly, he appeared to do most of the talking, with Summer just nodding her head now and again in response. The woman was nothing more than an airhead, Christie finally decided, with no conversation at all by the look of things. She almost felt sorry for Lucas. Almost.

Eventually Toby also lapsed into silence, and she felt his gaze resting upon her as for the umpteenth time her eyes were inexorably drawn toward Lucas.

'Christie — ' Toby's tone was one of irritation as he snapped his fingers in front of her. ' — for the third time, shall we go?'

'Oh, s-sorry, I was miles away.'

'Yes, and we know where. Somewhere most certainly not miles away,' he concluded in angry exasperation. 'In fact, you were just a few feet away — across the room.'

Christie dragged her glance back to him. 'Oh Toby, I'm sorry.'

'Don't be,' he bit out. 'I get the message. Loud and clear.' His expression challenged her to deny his insinuation.

'M-message?' she stammered, even though she knew very well what he meant.

'Yeah, you know, the one where you finish with me?'

'Oh Toby, I'm sorry,' she said again.

Strangely, he didn't look as anguished as she'd expected. Maybe his emotions weren't as fully engaged as she'd believed — or as he'd led her to believe.

'Yeah, you've already said.' He was actually pouting now, and sounding more like a boy than the man he was. A small boy, moreover, who'd discovered he couldn't have the particular toy that he'd coveted. She'd never seen this side of him before — but then again, she'd invariably gone along with whatever he'd suggested, so she supposed there'd been no need for such a display.

'I've been meaning to say something for a while.'

'Well, don't bother, Christie. As I said, I already get it. And if I'm honest, I have been expecting it in a way. You've always been cool towards me; cold, in fact, at times. It's been like kissing a bloody ice cube.'

His words stung. No man had ever said that to her before. Had she really been that cold? Was that her problem? Was she frigid? Was she never going to fall in love? 'There'll be someone else, I'm sure. Someone right for you, who'll love you as you need to be — '

'Don't patronize me. And, for your information, I don't like being strung along.'

Christie bent her head. She didn't know what to say. And what could she say, when all was said and done? He was right: she had been stringing him along. She should have ended things weeks ago. She'd known, even then, that there was no future for them. No wonder he was angry.

'I'm sorry.'

She'd said that so many times now, it was beginning to sound insincere. She became suddenly aware of the throbbing of a headache. She lifted a hand and gently massaged her temple. She couldn't argue with him. She looked back at him. He didn't look all that hurt. Angry, yes. His pride was probably dented. But hurt? Not really.

She sneaked a glance at Lucas then, only to discover him watching them, his interest only too plain. Did he realize what was happening?

'So will you be staying here?'

Christie shook her head and returned her glance to Toby. Of course, he'd noticed her sideways glance at Lucas and his subsequent expression revealed scornful contempt.

'Not permanently, no. I'm staying for the funeral and then I must get back, providing Grandmother's all right. There's my gallery to sort out.'

'They'll miss you,' he said, bitterness now lacing his tone.

'Well, my grandmother will. I don't know about anyone else.'

'Oh, I'm sure Lucas will,' he blurted almost spitefully.

Christie stared at him. 'L-Lucas?'

'Oh, come on. I'm not blind, Christie. You haven't been able to keep your eyes off him all evening, and he's sneaked quite a few looks at you.'

Christie's heart gave an involuntary leap. Lucas had been looking at her? When? She hadn't noticed.

Toby was still talking. 'Look, take a tip from me. Be careful with him. He looks as hard as nails. In which case, he'll only ever be out for number one — himself. So watch you don't get your fingers burnt, right? Because there's a real risk you will if you persist in playing with that particular brand of fire.'

8

'It isn't how you think,' Christie protested.

'Oh for God's sake, give me some credit. I'm not blind — or stupid, come to that,' Toby snapped. 'Admit it: it's him you really want, so I'm just to be dispensed with, got rid of, airbrushed out of the picture.' He once again snapped his fingers in the air. Several peoples' heads turned; eyes widened with curiosity as they realized what was going on. He thrust himself forward, leaning threateningly across the table towards her. 'I'm an inconvenience all of a sudden,' he hissed; droplets of saliva landed on her face. She flinched, resisting the urge to wipe them away. The gesture would only add to his fury. 'Well, thanks very much. As I've just said, you're cold, cold and hard; as hard as he is.' He leant even further across the table, until their heads were practically touching. 'Well, do you know what, Christie? You're welcome to each other. In fact — dare I say it — you deserve each other. I hope you'll be very happy — although from what I've seen of Lucas Grant, I very much doubt that.' Toby's face was brick-red by this time, his eyes blazing with fury. She didn't dare to look over to see what Lucas was making of this.

'Toby — please, people are staring. Let's continue this in the car.'

'No. You started it in here. We'll damn well finish it in here. Who cares who's looking?'

'I do.'

'Is everything all right here?'

Christie looked up. Lucas was standing there, looking down on them.

'Y-yes,' Christie stammered. Now it was her turn to flush crimson, and all she could think was, how mortifying was this? Whatever must he be thinking?

'Well if you don't mind me saying so,

it doesn't look it.' He swept his gaze to Toby. 'Toby?'

'Oh, clear off,' Toby spat. 'You've done more than enough as it is.'

Christie gasped in horror. 'Toby, don't — please.'

Lucas didn't say anything, other than to raise an eyebrow quizzically at Christie. But his expression told her beyond any doubt that he knew exactly what Toby meant; that she was more interested in Lucas than she was in him. And in that crushing second, Christie wanted nothing more than to be allowed to quietly die — right here, right now.

'Christie?' Lucas then gently said.

'It's all right, Lucas. Really.' She lurched to her feet. She couldn't stay here. Every eye in the place was now glued to the three of them, including Summer's. She was staring across at them, eyes wide, lips parted. 'We're just going. Toby?'

But Toby was already on his feet. 'I won't be seeing you again, Grant, so I'll say my goodbyes now.'

'Oh dear,' Lucas murmured. 'Leaving so soon?' His voice was perfectly smooth, his expression an untroubled one; a marked contrast to Toby's. He turned his gaze to Christie then. 'Is he safe to drive? Because — '

'Hey, I'm over here.' Toby slapped his hand against his chest, anger distorting his face; his mouth. 'Ask me, not her. Of course, I'm safe to drive.'

'Thanks, Lucas,' Christie softly said. 'We'll be fine.'

His eyes darkened as he regarded her, his eyelids lowered. 'Sure?'

She nodded. She felt almost too fragile to speak. And if he showed any more concern, she was afraid she'd burst into tears.

'Right. I'll see you tomorrow then.'

★ ★ ★

Toby left the next morning. Christie went into the village to say goodbye. She couldn't let him go in the mood that he was in. He'd been so furious with her the night before, ranting about Lucas and his arrogance — his sheer cheek — all the way back to Heron House.

'I mean, who the blazes does he think he is? Am I okay to drive, indeed. Does he think I'm stupid — huh? Stupid enough to drive while intoxicated?'

They'd parted in front of Heron House with the barest of civilities. Christie decided it was best to just let him go. 'I'll come and see you in the morning before you leave,' she called as she waved him off.

She thought she heard him mutter, 'Don't bother,' but she couldn't be sure.

Anyway, she was determined he shouldn't leave with such bad feeling between them, so the following morning she drove to the hotel early. So early, in fact, she was forced to wait for him in the reception area.

'I'm really sorry, Toby,' she again said when he finally appeared.

'Are you, Christie?'

'Yes, I am.'

'Well, I doubt I'll see you again, so I hope you'll be happy.'

He didn't look quite so furious this morning, leading her to once again suspect he wasn't as much in love with her as he'd said. And if that was the case, he'd soon find someone else; someone who'd love him and so make him a darned sight happier than she'd done.

'I'll try to be.'

'But I wouldn't bank on it with him,' he sneered. He was referring to Lucas, of course.

'Toby, it's really not how you think. You saw him; he's with someone else.'

'Yeah, right. If you believe he's with that-that bimbo, then you aren't as smart as I've always believed.' His look sharpened then. 'Face up to your feelings, Christie — your true feelings, and-and deal with them. Otherwise you'll never be happy.' And with those final words, he was gone.

His departure left Christie with a strong sense of abandonment which, she supposed, wasn't entirely unpredictable. Toby had been in her life for a while now. She'd got used to him being around, on the end of the phone line if she needed him. But he wasn't the one for her; she knew that — and so did he if, he was honest with himself. Which begged the question: who was right for her? She had no answer to that, or at least, not one that she wanted to hear. Lucas was at the house when she arrived back. Just Lucas, standing in the hallway. Normally he'd have left the house by now. Could Toby's scornful words have somehow conjured him up?

'Where is everyone?' she nervously asked him.

She'd hoped, in the wake of the embarrassing scene of the previous evening, that she would meet him for the first time with her family around her. Now, she asked herself, had he known she'd gone out and so had been waiting for her to return? That seemed unlikely, unless he'd been looking through a window and had seen her leaving. But if he had indeed been waiting for her, what did he want? He'd clearly sussed out what had been happening between Toby and her. Toby, for one, with his blunt words, had made it perfectly obvious what he'd been thinking: that it was Lucas in whom she was interested. Was that why he was waiting for her — to challenge her over it?

However, he must have decided to take pity on her because, despite the gleaming gaze that told her he was well aware of Toby's meaning, all he said was, 'Venetia is in her room still. Alice is having a walk in the garden.'

'Rafe?'

'Out. So that just leaves you and me.' He was watching her, his eyes mere slits. 'So, has he gone then?'

'Who?' She knew quite well who he meant.

'The Toby jug.'

'Don't be so rude!'

198

'Sorry. You're right, it was rude. Has he gone?'

'Yes.'

'After more passionate kisses, no doubt.'

'It's really none of your business.'

'Is it serious between you two?'

'Once again, none of your business.'

Undeterred by her forthrightness, he went on, 'It looked serious, judging by the kiss you exchanged upon his arrival. And what was going on last evening? You had the entire restaurant riveted. It was like watching a scene from a soap opera.' His gaze glittered with a hard light.

Was there no stopping this man? Did he have no shame, quizzing her in this bold fashion? 'For the third time, none of your business. And for your information, I was taken by surprise when he kissed me, that's all.'

'Really!' Gone was the hard look; instead, he looked positively delighted by her answer.

Christie glowered at him. What was

coming now? She didn't have to wait long to find out.

'Well, if that's the result of catching you by surprise I'll have to try it myself.'

'You wouldn't dare.' Which was a really, really stupid thing to say. She was quite sure there wasn't anything that Lucas wouldn't dare.

She was right. He began to move purposefully towards her. 'Is that a challenge, Christie?' Despite the fact that he was now dangerously close to her, his voice was so low she only just caught the words.

'N-no.' Swiftly she retreated, only to find her back pressed against the wall of the hallway with no way of escape.

'Are you sure of that? Because you should know I never, ever refuse a challenge when it's offered.'

'Y-yes, I'm sure.'

'You don't sound it.'

He was even closer now, too close; she could feel his breath feathering the skin of her face and smell his aftershave. It was a heady, intoxicating scent. She could see the glint of his eyes — the tiny, amber flecks. Her head swam; she swayed . . .

And suddenly his arms were about her, holding her steady; holding her close. Her breasts were pressed against him, as were her stomach and thighs. She quivered, achingly aware of the sheer power of him. He could do whatever he wanted with her and she would be unable to stop him.

'Steady,' he murmured huskily. 'You could fall.'

His lips were only a centimetre away. She gazed, helplessly at him; mesmerized. And then, she simply couldn't help herself. She tilted her head, and asked, 'What about Summer?'

'What about Summer?'

He was watching her intently now. She'd have to be careful; that narrowed gaze would miss nothing.

'Well — what would she think of this? After all, isn't she your girlfriend?'

His expression gave nothing away. 'No.'

'So what were you doing out with her?'

He didn't speak for a long, long moment. Then, 'I took her for a meal because she's new in town and her father asked me to. He's a business acquaintance. Now, can we stop talking about Summer?'

Her eyes widened and her lips parted as she let out a long, slow breath. So he wasn't involved with the other woman. Emotion surged deep within her.

She heard his low groan and then his muttered, 'And will you please stop looking at me like that?' right before his head swooped and his mouth captured hers: initially in a light touch, but then when she made no move to stop him, in a deeper, more passionate kiss. His tongue forced her lips apart and plunged within.

Christie didn't know what came over her then. But, powerless to prevent them, her hands moved up his chest and her fingers intertwined behind his head as they tangled themselves in

202

amongst the tendrils of his hair.

Again he groaned, throatily this time, and pulled her even closer; his breathing grew laboured as she became all too aware of the hardness of him, of his muscular body against her softer, feminine curves; his arousal. It felt so right. They felt so right — together. His hands began to move now too, tracing her curves, cupping them, caressing them. Her insides turned to molten fire. Was this what Toby had sensed growing between them? This desire, this passion? Even before she had?

He ground his mouth over hers, forcing her lips further apart. She gave a low moan. She wanted this man; there was no point in denying it any longer. And then, abruptly and way too soon, he ended the kiss and lifted his head to gaze down at her, his eyes burning into hers, his blazing passion on full display. She could hardly breathe.

And then, as he stared down at her, sanity returned. 'Wh-what are you doing?' she gasped.

'What am *I* doing?' He gave a snort of laughter. 'It does take two, you know, and I have to say, you didn't seem to mind. In fact, you were an eager participant — very eager,' he added softly.

'Well, yes,' she grudgingly and haltingly conceded, primly adding, 'but it's hardly the right time. So soon after my grandfather's death — '

'What the blazes is going on here?'

They sprang apart, for all the world like two guilty children caught in some unspeakable act. It was Rafe. Neither of them had heard the front door opening.

'What were you doing?'

'Um — ' Christie stammered. 'I had something in my eye.' She closed her eyes. Oh God! How lame was that? She opened her eyes again to see Lucas regarding her with bemused astonishment. But he did back her up. Although why she was so bothered about Rafe knowing they'd been kissing, she couldn't have said. Other than the fact that it was so soon — disrespectfully soon, in fact — after his father's death.

'Yes,' Lucas agreed with a wildly exaggerated solemnity, 'a piece of grit practically the size of a house brick. I think I've got it, though.' He proceeded to minutely inspect the tip of his index finger, before with an 'Aah, there it is,' he flicked off the imaginary grit.

Christie smothered a giggle. Surely Rafe would see through his play-acting? Lucas was smiling gently at her, which did absolutely nothing to help her state of mind. What it did do, however, was inspire a long, hard stare from Rafe.

But all he said was, 'Could I have a word, Lucas?'

'Sure. Now?'

'Yes. In private.' Rafe shot Christie a dark look, as if the entire episode had been her fault.

'Well, I'm on my way upstairs,' Lucas told him. 'Come with me to my apartment.' He glanced Christie's way. 'Sorry, Christie. We'll have to continue our, uh, business another time.'

Christie was thoroughly confused as

to his motive for kissing her. He wasn't seriously attracted to her, was he? Toby had certainly thought so. And his love-making had certainly seemed to suggest that possibility. One thing she did know, however — she was dangerously attracted to him and had responded with an equal passion to his. Which did disprove Toby's allegation and allay her own fear that she was cold; frigid, even.

She lingered in the hallway, her thoughts in turmoil as she reflected upon what had just happened. It meant she heard what Rafe said quite clearly.

'I need to borrow some money — quite a lot of money. I'm in a spot of bother. I wouldn't normally ask you, but I can't bring myself to ask Mother. She'll blow another gasket.'

She didn't hear Lucas's response because by that time they'd moved too far away. But she did wonder why Rafe needed to borrow a lot of money. His cost of living wouldn't be high, surely. He still lived at home. And she didn't imagine he paid any of the household bills, or even contributed to them. Not if her grandmother's frequent and disparaging remarks were to be believed.

She walked up the stairs after them, her head bowed in thought. Maybe Venetia had good reason to complain about Rafe's scrounging off her. He obviously spent money he didn't possess.

She reached her bedroom and opened the door. And what she saw within drove everything else from her head: Lucas's lovemaking, her own heated response, Rafe's request for money.

For each of the paintings and sketches that she had so carefully executed had been torn from the pad and ripped up before being scattered around the room, while across the dressing table mirror was scrawled, in what looked like her most expensive lipstick, the words 'Go away. You're not wanted here.'

9

Christie walked slowly into the room and sank down onto her bed, her heart pounding, as she viewed the comprehensive destruction of her work.

Who could have done this? Rafe?

In the light of Samson's antics outside her bedroom door, he was the most likely candidate. After all, the dog had looked ready to leap at her; possibly attack her. If her uncle had been behind that, as she'd believed at the time, then it stood to reason that he was the one behind this too. But why would he do such things?

The answer presented itself almost immediately. The words left no room for doubt, none at all. Someone — Rafe? — wanted her to leave, to go away and never return; and frightening her and then destroying her work was likely to be the most effective way of achieving that.

But he'd been out, hadn't he? She'd seen him come back in. Or had he inflicted the damage before he'd gone? Could he, too, have seen her leaving the house? If he had, he'd have had ample time, because the destruction, as complete as it had been, wouldn't have taken more than a few minutes. He could then have left the house, thereby creating a credible alibi for himself.

Or, as much as she was loath to consider such a thing, could Lucas be the culprit? Could he and Rafe even be scheming together? She was fairly sure that Lucas had been in the house throughout her absence.

Yet, looked at realistically, it had to be Rafe who was responsible. He had the most reason for trying to drive her away; the most to gain. And if she left suddenly — after her grandmother had specifically asked her to stay — the old lady, in her grief, might be so disappointed in her that she'd disinherit Christie and all the wealth would revert to Rafe. That theory seemed a much better bet than the damage being down to Lucas. He wouldn't inherit anything much on Venetia's death. No, her subconscious whispered, but he might on Rafe's; therefore, wasn't it reasonable to suppose that he would be as keen as Rafe to restore the inheritance to the person they deemed its rightful recipient? And as for Lucas's love-making, could that have been a calculated bid to divert suspicion away from himself? A masterly piece of play-acting? He'd already proved himself capable of such deceit by his oh-so-convincing pretence of removing a piece of grit from her eye.

She frowned. But whoever it had been, one or both of them, they couldn't be sure that she wouldn't tell her grandmother what had happened and, by so doing, thwart their plan. Because Venetia would almost certainly do her utmost to discover who was behind it. Or had they gambled on Christie not wishing to cause more worry for Venetia at such a sad time, trusting she would simply leave without any sort of explanation?

Well, whoever it was needed to think again, because she refused to be driven away. And whoever it was behind the destruction of her work had to be made to realize that. Maybe then, if he knew he was on a hiding to nothing, he wouldn't try anything else.

Her grandfather's funeral had been set for two days hence.

Christie had intended to remain for that. Now she resolved to remain even longer, to provide comfort for her grandmother if nothing else. Lengthening her stay would also send out a clear message that she wasn't going to be driven away; her gallery could wait.

So that evening at dinner she announced, 'Grandmother, I've decided to stay on for a while after the funeral, if that's okay?'

'Oh, Christie, of course it is,' Venetia instantly and warmly responded. 'That would be most kind of you.'

Christie watched closely for any sign

of anger or resentment in either Lucas or Rafe, but saw nothing other than a barely noticeable tightening of her uncle's jaw as he glared at her, which could have signified nothing more troubling than exasperation. In fact, she saw nothing to cause her actual fear.

Yet, his wretched dog had looked ready to attack her the other night. Should she say something to him? Not here, though, in front of everyone. She'd catch him on his own and threaten to tell her grandmother if he didn't exert some control over his pet. And if that made her seem like a juvenile then so be it.

*   *   *

The funeral passed without incident, apart from the sounds of Alice weeping into her lace hankie. Venetia did at one point lean forward and gently admonish, 'Alice, if I can control myself, you should be able to.'

Christie, who was sitting between

Venetia and Alice, took hold of her aunt's hand and squeezed it. She did seem disproportionately upset. Maybe she'd been fonder of Victor than anyone had imagined.

Rafe and Lucas sat side-by-side, granite-jawed and dry-eyed, although once or twice she observed the flexing of a muscle in Lucas's cheek. So maybe he wasn't as unmoved as he appeared. Certainly, after Rafe's distress the day his father died, she'd expected some show of grief from him, however small. But maybe he was suppressing it, not wishing to display his deeper emotions for all and sundry to see. And there were a lot of people in the small church; so many that the pews had quickly filled, forcing a number of mourners to stand against the walls of the nave. Her grandfather had obviously been a much respected man.

For her part, she was heartily glad when it was all over. She hadn't actually given way to tears, but she'd come very close more than once, her throat aching painfully with the effort of suppression. They returned to the house where Delia had laid out a buffet for any mourners who wished to refresh themselves before returning to their homes. None turned up, however, and it wasn't long before Delia could be heard muttering, 'Wicked waste of good food,' as she busily tidied everything away again.

Within a day or two things had reverted more or less to normal. It was only Christie who couldn't settle. She hadn't known her grandfather for very long but in that short time she'd grown to love him, and she missed him; missed his gentle smile, his readiness to listen.

In a bid to escape the house and her feeling of sadness, Christie took herself off to the village. She didn't feel that she was abandoning her grandmother; the old lady had gone upstairs for her afternoon rest and anyway she wasn't going to be long. Once there she quickly spotted a café situated on the edge of a small square, with each of its outside tables carefully positioned to catch every single ray of sunlight. She settled herself at one of these and ordered a cappuccino coffee and an ice cream.

She was sitting, face turned up to the warmth, when she sensed someone watching her. A middle-aged woman. She nodded at Christie, smiling as she did so. Suddenly she stood up and walked over. 'Excuse me, but I have to ask. Are you Laura and Adam's daughter? Only I'd heard you were here.'

Christie smiled now too. 'Yes, I'm Christie. Please — ' She indicated the chair opposite her. ' — won't you sit down?'

Laura had never mentioned anyone from her old life — well, she wouldn't have if she'd intended to keep her past a secret. And Christie had found nothing amongst her papers to suggest she'd kept in touch with anyone from Devon, apart from the three letters from Venetia.

'Um, I don't . . . '

'I'm sorry, I should have introduced myself. I'm Jennifer Holby. Your mum and I were close friends when she lived here.'

'Oh, I see.'

'I heard about Adam and now poor Laura. You must be missing her terribly. I regret to say we lost touch years ago.'

So if Jennifer knew about her parents' deaths and now Christie's unexpected arrival, someone must have been talking, Christie decided. Delia, probably.

Jennifer grinned, obviously reading her thoughts. 'You know what these small villages are like.'

'I didn't, but I'm learning.'

'So how do you like it — staying at the house?'

'It's been great to spend time with my grandparents,' she prevaricated, thus avoiding having to give a direct answer. She could hardly tell a complete stranger how tense things were, at least with regards to Rafe. 'You've heard about my grandfather dying?'

216

'Yes. I was sorry about that too. He used to be a familiar figure around the village before he had his stroke. Not like Rafe. We barely glimpse him.' There was an infinitesimal pause and then, 'I don't mean to pry, but . . . how do you get along with him?'

'I haven't actually seen much of him,' Christie again diplomatically replied. Not that that wasn't perfectly true. She'd been hoping to see him to complain about Samson but, since the funeral, she hadn't as much as glimpsed him. Neither him nor his horrible dog.

'I heard that no one knew of your existence before you showed up on the doorstep.'

Delia once again, Christie guessed; none of the family would have talked, she was sure, given their preference for seclusion. She just hoped Venetia didn't find out that her housekeeper had been gossiping about family affairs. It could mean instant dismissal, knowing her grandmother as Christie had come to.

'I bet Rafe hated your appearing

from nowhere, didn't he? It's common knowledge he only stayed so he'd inherit everything eventually. Whereas now — ' She eyed Christie speculatively. ' — he'll probably find himself having to share.'

Christie didn't respond. The family's financial affairs were no one else's business, and she certainly wasn't going to provide fuel for further gossip.

'Rafe — ' Jennifer again hesitated. ' — isn't very well liked hereabouts.'

Christie stared at her.

'I'm sorry. Maybe I shouldn't have said anything.'

'No, please.' Christie had belatedly realized that here was the very person to tell her about her mother's life with Rafe. With Jennifer and Laura being such good friends, it was very likely her mother would have confided in her. 'You see, I don't really know why my mother's marriage to Rafe ended in the way it did. Why she deserted him for my father. My parents never spoke about the family or their lives here. My mother only told me about them when she knew she was dying. And she was too weak to say all that much. I didn't want to press her about it.'

'Oh, I see.' Jennifer looked startled by this piece of information, so obviously Delia had kept some things to herself. 'Well, Rafe treated your mother shockingly badly.'

'You don't mean he hit her?' Christie gasped. That was something she hadn't considered — physical abuse.

Jennifer frowned. 'I don't think so. She never said he did and I'm sure she would have told me. No, it wasn't anything like that; it was the way he was never at home. She was stuck in that house with just his parents, Alice, and of course Adam. What happened was inevitable in my opinion.'

'Why didn't my grandparents ever say anything to Rafe? They must have seen what was happening.'

'Well according to your mother, for all Venetia's bossiness she could be very good at turning a blind eye to certain

219

things. She had — has — an almost pathological hatred for gossip, and the thought that people might talk about them. I wondered at the time whether she thought that if she just ignored the situation it would disappear. Only, of course, it didn't. So when Adam and Laura went off together, it was inevitable that she would blame them for everything, not Rafe. Although I think she's come round since then and has long realized that Rafe was largely to blame.'

Jennifer was eyeing her again, Christie noticed. She seemed undecided about something. Christie wondered if she was debating saying more or whether to remain silent.

However, indiscretion must have won out because she said, 'Has anyone told you about Rafe's gambling?' The words erupted in an explosion, almost as if she wanted to get the bad things over with as quickly as possible.

'Gambling?' Christie exclaimed.

'Yes.' Again, she seemed undecided

about continuing. 'I don't know whether I should say anything . . . '

'Oh, please. It will be in the strictest confidence, naturally.'

That must have reassured Jennifer, because she went on, 'We-ell, it wasn't just his neglect that made your mum leave. He gambled practically all their money away. Laura worked hard to pay their way and Rafe would take every penny he could get his hands on, even stealing from her purse on a couple of occasions, and put it all on a horse or a game of cards. Why, I've known him gamble on whether it would rain for a particular occasion or snow at Christmas. She was in despair.'

The pieces were all slotting into place for Christie. Rafe still gambled. That was why Venetia despised him; why Christie had heard him asking to borrow money from Lucas. Yet Lucas must know what he was doing. Why did he give him anything? Or maybe he didn't. She didn't actually know the outcome of the request that she'd overheard.

'Your mother tried to talk to Venetia about it, but Venetia refused to discuss it — wouldn't even listen to Laura.'

But surely, Christie mused, her grandmother must have had some inkling of what was going on at the time? Must have realized it was Laura footing the couple's bills? She was far from stupid. That had to be why Venetia had eventually written asking Adam and Laura to return home. Because, as Jennifer said, she'd discovered — or rather, finally, admitted — what Rafe had been doing while he was married to Laura.

No wonder Venetia didn't want him to have all the family money to gamble away, in all likelihood. Christie's arrival had provided her with a valid reason to alter her and Victor's will.

* * *

It was two days later, while everyone was gathered in the sitting room after dinner, that Venetia announced that one of her more valuable pieces of jewellery was missing. An antique emerald and diamond brooch. Christie's first thought was that Lucas had refused to lend him any money, so Rafe had taken it to try and raise what he needed. But knowing her son as she did, surely Venetia would also suspect that?

However, it would seem not. Because when Lucas asked, 'When did you last see it, Venetia?' Venetia replied, without as much as a glance at Rafe, 'Well, let me see. Tssk.' She shook her head impatiently. 'How can I be expected to remember with everything that's happened? It's gone now, that's all that's relevant. Apart from its monetary value, it has enormous sentimental value. It was my grandmother's. It was her wedding gift from my grandfather. She passed it on to my mother and my mother gave it to me. I think we should call the police. We may have had a burglary.'

'But if we've had a burglary, surely they'd have taken other things too,'

Lucas pointed out. 'There's plenty of silver dotted about, all easily portable. I haven't noticed anything missing. Plus, surely there'd be signs of a break-in.'

'Hmm,' Venetia murmured. 'I must have just mislaid it. In that case . . . '

It was then that she glanced sideways at Rafe, her belated suspicion plain to Christie if no one else. She must have decided not to openly accuse him, however. Out of family loyalty? If it was, then it would surely be a first. Or maybe she hoped that if she ignored the suspicion, it wouldn't turn out to be true. After all, it wouldn't be a pleasant thing to suspect that your son had stolen from you.

Delia, who had come into the room carrying a tray of coffee and had obviously heard enough to know what had happened, intervened. 'Let Matt and me search the house thoroughly, Mrs Wakeham. Everywhere — the bedrooms, as well, providing nobody minds, of course.' Upon receiving no sounds of protest from any quarter, she went on, 'Before you take the drastic step of calling the police. As you say, you've probably just mislaid it; put it somewhere and forgotten.'

'Good idea, Delia. Have a thorough look. No one will mind.' Her determined glance around challenged anyone to dispute that.

'Grandmother, I seem to recall you were wearing an emerald brooch the day I arrived. I remember thinking how beautiful it was. I haven't seen you wear it since.'

'You're right, Christie. I remember now. And I'm sure — ' She frowned as if still in doubt. ' — almost sure I replaced it in my jewellery box. So if that's the case, why isn't it still there?'

'Well, you know what I think, Mother,' Rafe chipped in. 'You shouldn't be keeping a thing of such value in a box that anyone can open.'

'And who asked for your opinion, Rafe?' Venetia demanded to know.

As she invariably did, Alice sprang to Rafe's defence. 'Venetia, Rafe has every right, as your only living son to — '

'Oh, do be quiet, Alice. Delia, I wish you to search every room, irrespective of whose it is,' Venetia instructed. She again looked at Rafe, making Christie wonder if she suspected that he had it concealed somewhere until he could sell it. It would seem so, because her next words were, 'We will all wait here until you have done so.'

Her intentions were only too clear. She didn't want Rafe rushing away to retrieve the brooch before Delia or Matt could discover it amongst his belongings — providing he hadn't already sold it of course, in which case it wouldn't be found.

10

Once Delia had left the room to go in search of both Matt and the missing brooch, Christie tentatively asked her grandmother, 'You don't think one of them could have taken it, do you?' She hated having to accuse anyone, but nobody seemed to have considered that possibility. The pair would have the perfect opportunity, after all, having unsupervised access to all the rooms — especially Delia, in the course of her daily work.

'Well, if it was, you can be assured that the possibility of the police being called will be all that's needed to ensure they find it quickly.'

'Of course it isn't Delia or Matt,' Alice burst out. 'They're as honest as the day. Good heavens, they've been with you for twenty years, Venetia.'

'If you ask me,' Rafe then put in, 'it's rather odd that the last time the brooch

227

was definitely seen was on the day that Christie arrived.'

Venetia glowered at him. 'And what's that supposed to mean? Are you accusing my granddaughter of theft?'

Rafe turned an even deeper puce than he normally was. 'N-no, of-of course not. I just thought it seems a bit of a coincidence, that's all.'

'Well, kindly keep your thoughts to yourself,' Venetia snapped.

Christie felt her heartbeat quicken along with the first faint stirring of unease. Rafe was trying to throw suspicion onto her. And it was working. Lucas and Alice had both turned their gazes towards her.

'Christie?'

Wary of what she might now glimpse in his eye, Christie turned to look at Lucas, bracing herself for some sort of accusation.

But 'No one believes that you took the brooch,' was all he said. 'Rafe didn't mean that — did you, Rafe?' Lucas turned his head to look at Rafe, his expression steely.

'No, goodness me. Certainly not. I was just — '

But whatever he was about to say to try and redeem himself was cut short by the return of Delia, this time with Matt. Delia mutely held out the brooch.

'Where was it?' Venetia asked, taking it from her. 'In my bedroom, after all?'

Delia glanced at Christie, her expression a strange one. 'No. I'm sorry, Miss Wakeham . . . '

Christie felt as if the floor was shifting beneath her.

'It was in your room, in a drawer amongst your undergarments.'

'Don't be ridiculous, Delia,' Venetia boomed. 'Why should Christie have it in her room?'

'Hah!' shouted Rafe. 'Just as I suspected.'

'Be quiet, Rafe,' Venetia commanded. 'If anyone took it, it would have been you.' Thus she put her unspoken suspicion into words for all to hear.

★ ★ ★

Christie sat in her bedroom, stunned and shaking. She'd fled in the wake of the discovery of the brooch in her drawer, ignoring Venetia's anguished cry of, 'Christie . . . '

Rafe had done this to her, she was positive. He had planted the brooch amongst her things to make everyone believe she'd stolen it. He'd even put the accusation into words, more or less.

Was he so disappointed that his destruction of her paintings had failed to drive her away that he had resorted to making her look like a thief, in the hope that her grandmother would believe that and send her away in disgrace? Yet Venetia had called out to her as she'd fled. Did that mean that she knew that Christie wasn't capable of such a thing?

If it was Rafe responsible and he'd failed yet again — this time, in an attempt to discredit her in front of the whole family — what would he try next?

It was then that she recalled his warning. 'The moor can be a very dangerous place. Lots of bogs, fast-running rivers, nasty things like that. Wouldn't want you to trip into one. You could be badly — even fatally — injured.' But surely he wouldn't try to actually harm her — would he? She was his niece, for God's sake . . .

As her heart gave a lurch, a knock came on the door and Venetia's voice called, 'Christie, can I come in?'

'Yes.'

She stared at the door as it opened. She wouldn't be able to bear it if her grandmother's expression was an accusing one.

But that fear was swiftly dispelled, because her grandmother's first words were, 'I know it wasn't you.'

'How? You barely know me,' Christie whispered. 'The others probably think it was me.' Even Lucas, she was sure, despite his earlier unexpected show of support of her.

'No, they don't. We all agree that somehow it ended up in your drawer by accident. I've been thinking. There's only one explanation as far as I can see. I must have worn the brooch again, after you saw it that first day, and obviously it fell off somewhere, somehow. Delia laundered some of your things, didn't she? The brooch must have got tangled amongst them, and-and Delia, not noticing, replaced it along with your clean garments in your drawer.'

Christie regarded her grandmother with astonishment. Did she really believe such a preposterous theory? Maybe she should tell her right now what she thought — that Rafe had planted the brooch in an attempt to portray her as a thief after his previous attempt to drive her away had failed. But no, she couldn't do that. How could she accuse her uncle of such things? And, moreover, with no proof?

'I think it's best that I leave. I'm only causing more friction between you and Rafe.'

'Do you want everyone to believe you stole the brooch? Because that's precisely what they will think if you run away.'

'You're right,' Christie miserably conceded. She had to stay.

She didn't mention the destruction of her paintings, however, or the writing on the mirror.

*   *   *

But the following day, she wondered whether she should simply accept that her guilt would be assumed, and leave forthwith. No one had mentioned the brooch again, not even Rafe. Which, in a strange sort of way, made her feel even worse.

She decided, in a desperate attempt to escape the oppressive atmosphere that existed within the house, to pay a second visit to the nearby village. Having stayed longer than she'd intended at Heron House, there were several things that she needed; she hoped one of the few shops that she'd seen there on her previous visit would stock them. But more than that, she hoped that the distraction, as tedious as she invariably found shopping to be, would banish the nightmarish events of the previous day from her mind.

Her suspicions kept returning to Rafe. He was the only one with a real motive, wasn't he? And he kept directing glances her way that could only be described as triumphant. If it hadn't been him behind it, then things were certainly going his way.

And it wasn't only Rafe who was behaving in a strange manner. Alice had taken to gazing at her for several moments at a time, her expression one of troubled uncertainty, her handkerchief fluttering and waving before she finally pressed it to her trembling lips; it was as if she were trying to physically ward off her growing suspicion. At least Venetia was convinced of Christie's innocence. She couldn't have borne it if her grandmother had also demonstrated doubt about her.

As for Lucas . . . well, Lucas, after his avowal that nobody believed her to have taken the brooch, hadn't said very much at all. She'd sensed him staring at her more than once; but when she'd glanced over at him, his expression was one of total impassivity.

Delia, like Alice, didn't appear to know what to think. She'd apologised afterwards for searching through Christie's personal belongings. All Christie had replied was, 'You were only doing what you had to, Delia — but I hope you believe me when I say that I didn't put the brooch in the drawer.' She didn't repeat Venetia's outlandish theory that somehow Delia had picked it up with the clean laundry. It might sound as if she were accusing the housekeeper.

Once she reached the shops, Christie purchased the items that she needed, a new lipstick being one of her priorities. The one she'd brought with her was now a mere stub. Luckily, the small general store seemed to stock almost everything that anyone could possibly need. The only drawback to that was, that in order to keep such a variety of goods, the shelves had to be placed so close together it made walking between them an obstacle course. Nonetheless, it didn't take Christie long to fill a large basket. Once she'd paid for it all, she decided to return to the café that she'd been to before and have a drink. Not because she was thirsty, but because she simply couldn't face going back to Heron House. Not yet.

She found an empty table and ordered a cappuccino coffee. She made it last as long as she could, but eventually of course she had no alternative but to return to the house.

She opened the front door, which never seemed to be locked, and stepped inside. It wasn't until she began to turn around from closing the door again that she heard the deep throated growl. She looked down and there was Samson just a couple of feet away from her, his mouth partly open, his teeth bared. She stopped breathing as she instinctively pressed her back against the door, trying to get as far away from him as possible. His hackles were raised and his eyes were glittering rapaciously.

She glanced wildly around. Where the hell was Rafe? Usually wherever the

236

dog was, he was somewhere nearby. Could he be hiding, watching, relishing her terror? She stared down at the dog. He had crept closer and wasn't just growling now; he was snarling. In fact, he was foaming at the mouth, the drool hanging in strips.

'Samson,' she stammered, 'it's me, Christie. You know me.'

The dog ignored her soft words, continuing to draw closer, his snarls growing more threatening with every second. She could feel his hot breath on her legs.

'Stop — sit — sit — ple-ease.'

Her voice shook, which was the wrong way entirely to control an animal like this. He needed to recognize that she was the boss, not him.

In desperation, she put an arm behind her, groping for the door handle, hoping she could make it outside before the animal could reach her. The problem with that was she couldn't get hold of it, not without turning around; it was too high. And in any case, she'd have to move closer to Samson before she could open the door wide enough to escape.

He inched forward again, his yellow teeth in full view. She could already feel the agony of them digging into her flesh, ripping, tearing . . .

She moved her bag to the front of her. If it came to it, she could use it as some sort of shield. 'Oh God, someone . . . help . . . please . . . '

When no one responded to her cries, she yelled even louder. But all that achieved was to make the dog snarl with yet more ferocity. His mouth looked ready to clamp itself round her leg when Rafe's voice finally delivered salvation. 'Samson — here, boy. That's enough. You've made your point.'

The dog instantly backed off, moving obediently to his master's side. Christie all but collapsed in relief, wrapping her arms about herself as she succumbed to muted sobs.

'Oh dear, has he frightened you?' Rafe laughed. 'He's harmless, really. It's all show. He just feels the need occasionally to strut his stuff. Prove he can still terrify someone.' He chuckled again. 'And he clearly had no trouble achieving that with you.'

Christie stared at him, her tears drying on her cheeks. He'd actually enjoyed watching her being frightened half to death. What a contemptible man he was. No wonder his mother despised him.

'He should be muzzled,' she yelled, fury having replaced the fear. 'He tried to get into my bedroom the other night — did you know that? He's-he's mad — dangerous. You just keep him away from me in future — you hear me?'

'That'll be a bit difficult, seeing as you inhabit the same house as him. Maybe you should leave. He was here first, after all.'

'I'll leave when I'm good and ready, and not a second before. So you can give up trying to frighten me; it's not going to work.' And she stalked past him and his horrid dog to swiftly ascend the stairs, eager now to place as much distance as she could between herself and the two of them. At last, he'd actually spoken the words 'maybe you should leave', proving, beyond all doubt he wanted her gone.

She sped along the landing to her bedroom and flung the door open, almost leaping inside in her haste to reach safety. She then slammed it shut. If there'd been a key, she'd have turned it and be blowed to any questions as to why she was locking herself in.

She stood for a moment then, her forehead resting against the wood, as she fought to calm her breathing and regain her composure. Which meant it wasn't until she straightened and turned into the room that she saw it.

She dropped the bag that she'd somehow kept hold of throughout everything, oblivious to the sounds of things clinking ominously, and covered her mouth with her hands. She gave a low moan. 'No . . . no.' It was too much, especially in the immediate aftermath of her terrifying ordeal with Samson.

She looked around. The devastation was even worse than last time, and she wouldn't have believed that possible. Every one of her tubes of oil paints had been removed from their box and were strewn around the room; some of the tops had been unscrewed and the contents squeezed over the surface of the dressing table and across the mirror; drawers stood open and her garments had been thrown onto the floor. Some of them also had paint smeared onto the fabric. Even the watercolours had been dug out of their small pans and crumbled haphazardly over the carpet, and the sketchpad that she'd left on her bed had had its pages torn out and then been ripped into small pieces. Fortunately there were only a couple of sketches inside, as she'd not had the time to do any more.

Swiftly she checked the top of the wardrobe, where she'd left a spare pad lying flat. That was intact, as were her boxes of charcoals, pastels and pencils. Clearly whoever it had been hadn't looked up there.

She plumped down onto the bed and gazed around the room. One question, and one question only, hammered away within her head. If this was down to her uncle — and she was becoming more and more convinced that it was — then he must genuinely hate her. He was obviously desperate to drive her away in disgrace, if it had been him who'd also planted the brooch in her drawer. Well, he'd seriously underestimated her. As she'd just told him, she'd only go when she was good and ready and not a second before.

But as she set about clearing the mess up, she asked herself, was it time to tell her grandmother what was happening? After all, if it was indeed Rafe, he was growing steadily more destructive; more daring. Even going as far as setting Samson onto her. Although he had called the animal off, could she rely on him doing that next time?

But what would the consequences be if she did tell Venetia? She had a strong suspicion that her grandmother would take her side against her son, with or without evidence to substantiate the accusation. He'd deny it, naturally. But apart from that, Christie really didn't want to be the one to come, maybe irrevocably, between mother and son.

So with all that in mind, she decided to stay silent for now, but nonetheless keep her guard up. Because as much as she didn't want to think it, she still wasn't one hundred percent sure that Lucas wasn't somehow involved in it all; although as he was probably at work, it was unlikely that he was responsible for this mess.

But no matter how she tried to convince herself that he wasn't the one tormenting her, the doubts stubbornly lingered. So when he stopped her at the foot of the stairs the next morning and asked, 'Christie, will you come out with me for the day? It's Saturday, so I don't need to go to the office,' she didn't know what to say. She couldn't help but think that if she said yes, she could be going out with the person who was plotting so cruelly against her. On the other hand, if he was with her, and the culprit had another go at destroying her belongings, well then she'd know it wasn't Lucas.

Unless, as she'd asked herself once before, could Lucas and Rafe be collaborating? Rafe doing the scary stuff, and Lucas . . . well, Lucas could be softening her up with his lovemaking in order to eventually persuade her to reject the inheritance.

Yet, despite all this agonizing, she heard herself saying, 'I'd like that.' And she admitted that she really would, despite her lingering doubts about his true intentions.

'Good,' he said, smiling with devastating charm. 'I thought a drive over Dartmoor and then lunch at a pub I know. Then afterwards, well, we'll see.' The gleam in his eyes set her pulse racing and the blood tingling through her veins. She even felt the heat of a blush rising up her face. Lucas, of course, noticed and the gleam intensified.

'I'd better let Grandmother know where — '

'I've already told her we're going out.'

Christie narrowed her eyes at him. Had he now? 'You must have been very confident I'd agree.' Even she could hear the indignation in her voice at his presumption, so he must be able to.

He had. He shrugged and gave a wry grin. 'No, simply optimistic.'

Christie's indignation vanished. What sort of power was this man exerting over her and her emotions? It was a sobering question, and one she didn't have the answer to.

'I hope you don't mind.'

To her astonishment, she found she didn't.

★   ★   ★

Which was how, within a very short space of time, she found herself seated at Lucas's side in his Mercedes convertible, top open, as they covered the moorland roads at a surprisingly modest speed. She'd have had Lucas down as a fast driver. Competent, as he would be at most things, she suspected, but fast.

'How's the painting coming along?' He slanted a quizzical glance her way.

She stiffened. How did he know she'd been painting? As far as she was aware he'd never seen her at work. Could it, after all, have been him responsible for the destruction in her room? She turned her head and met his gaze. His expression revealed nothing more disturbing than curiosity. 'Fine. How do you know I've been painting?'

'I saw you from my bedroom window.'

She wished he'd remove his gaze from her and concentrate on the road ahead. Luckily there was no other traffic, otherwise she was quite sure they'd have hit something by now. Maybe she should tell him what was happening to her and see how he reacted.

But when he unexpectedly veered to the left and pulled the car to a halt in a convenient lay-by and said, 'Let's walk, shall we?', she accepted that the moment had passed.

'Is that water I can hear?' she asked as she climbed from the car.

'Yes, there's a river over there.' He pointed again to the left of them. 'Do you want to have a look? If we're very lucky we might see a kingfisher. It's one of their favourite haunts. It would make a marvellous painting. Have you brought a camera?'

She nibbled at her bottom lip. She'd forgotten — again. 'No, sadly.'

They walked for a couple of hundred yards and there was the water she'd heard. A river, crystal-clear and almost torrential, rushing over a bed of small rocks and pebbles, its bank grassy and temptingly shaded from the unexpectedly hot sun by a row of tall trees. Poplars, she thought.

Christie sank down onto it, leaning back against one of the tree trunks. All of a sudden she felt incredibly and uncharacteristically weary — the undoubted result of disrupted sleep as she continually replayed all that had been happening to her. But all of that disappeared as Lucas stretched out by the side of her, propping himself up on one elbow to look at her. The sun dappled his face through the murmuring leaves, softening features that could at times be harsh. She felt a shiver of desire.

He regarded her thoughtfully. 'You look tired. Not sleeping well?'

'Not really, no.'

'Not surprising, considering recent events. It must have all come as a bit of a shock to you. Your mother dying, discovering a family you didn't know you had, losing the grandfather you'd barely had time to get to know.'

Caught off guard by this display of a gentler, more compassionate side to him, tears stung Christie's eyes. 'Yes, it has all been a bit traumatic. When I knew my mother was dying, I thought I was going to be totally alone.' Her voice broke as a single tear broke free and tracked its way down her face. She

248

dashed it away, angry with herself for this belated show of weakness. She wasn't generally the weepy sort. In fact, she despised women who resorted to crying the minute things got tricky. But despite her best efforts to control herself, more tears followed, until she was sobbing, quietly but uncontrollably, as in one massive outpouring she released the stress of the past days — well, weeks really — what with her mother's illness and subsequent death, finding out she had a previously unheard-of family, and travelling here to meet them. And then, everything that had been happening to her since.

Lucas instantly sat up and, reaching out a hand, used his thumb to gently stroke the tears away. 'I'm sorry. I shouldn't have mentioned anything.'

'No, it's okay. Really.'

'No, it isn't.' He sat up and moved closer to slide an arm about her, pulling her close, tucking her into his side.

Wordlessly, she shook her head as the tears began once more. 'I'm s-so s-sorry,' she eventually managed to stammer. 'I'm not usually like this.' She hiccupped helplessly.

'I know. Oh God, Christie,' she heard him mutter. He turned her to face him, cupping her chin with one hand. 'Don't — please don't.' But in the next instant, his words petered out as his mouth came down on hers.

Christie froze at first, but then, just like last time, she found herself kissing him back. His arms tightened about her, pulling her close, as her hands crept up his chest. Her fingers once again tangled themselves in amongst the strands of his hair as her lips parted and her breathing quickened. She heard someone moan and realized it was her. Yet somehow she couldn't stop.

What on earth was she doing? She knew this was wrong, so why was she behaving so wantonly? She knew nothing about Lucas, not really. Yet, for all that, the minute that he pressed her backwards and deepened the kiss, his tongue flicking against hers, she instantly responded; she couldn't help herself.

His hands began to move over her, caressing, tracing her curves — and suddenly, she was lying flat with him leaning over her, his mouth leaving hers to trace a pathway down her arched throat, finding the pulse that throbbed at the base, before his lips continued on down, searching out the shadowy cleft between her breasts and pressing his lips into it. Her body arched violently against his as passion took over. His hand crept beneath her top, finding and fondling her breast. Their legs intertwined as her breathing quickened and every nerve ending that she possessed became enflamed.

'Christie,' he groaned, 'you're so lovely . . . '

But it was as if the sound of his voice restored her sanity. She was behaving like a cheap tramp. She pushed him away. How could she? She didn't even know if she could trust him, for heaven's sake.

'Don't. Stop. What do you think

you're doing?' she foolishly gasped.

He grinned down at her. 'That's the second time you've asked me that. What do you think I'm doing?'

'Taking advantage?' she snapped, pulling herself completely free of his grasp and hurriedly sitting up, straightening her top as she did so.

'Taking advantage!' he exclaimed. 'All I did was try and comfort you. Okay, so things ran away with us.' His grin vanished and a steely look crept into his eye at her look of disgust, as much with herself as with him. 'Christie, it's perfectly natural for a man to want to kiss a beautiful woman.'

'Is that all it is?' she muttered.

'What do you mean?' He frowned at her.

It was then that the words burst from her, words that she'd barely thought, let alone intended saying. 'Well, my grandmother's will ensures that one day I'll be a reasonably wealthy woman, and you have to admit until recently you didn't exactly welcome me with open arms.

Not until after Grandmother changed her will, in fact.'

His eyes narrowed dangerously. 'What the hell are you implying?'

'Work it out for yourself.'

'You think I'm after whatever money you eventually inherit, is that it?' He gave a savage laugh.

She shrugged.

'Because I can assure you I don't need anyone else's wealth. I've got more than enough of my own.'

Christie scrambled to her feet. She'd said too much — again. Her and her big mouth. In which case, it might be wiser to put a bit of space between them.

But he too stood up, to tower threateningly over her. 'So is that what you really think? That I'm a fortune-hunter? You don't have much confidence in your own attraction then?' His tone was one of irony, though, not threat, and — contempt, she belatedly realized. Contempt for her.

Christie didn't answer; she daren't.

253

She'd said more than enough already.

His face paled and his jaw clenched; even his fists balled. For a split second, she thought he was about to strike her. 'What a very poor opinion you have of me.' His words flailed her. As did the look in his eyes. 'Well, we'll go home, shall we? After all, you won't want to spend time with someone you clearly have down as a cold-hearted gold-digger.'

He'd obviously forgotten that he'd once implied the very same thing about her. Silently, miserably, she followed him back to the car.

Had she got it all wrong? But much more to the point, had she just ruined any chance of getting close to Lucas? Because he was never going to forgive her for this. Never.

11

Christie saw nothing of Lucas over the next few days. Like Rafe, he appeared to have gone to ground somewhere. Avoiding her? She wouldn't be surprised, considering what she'd accused him of.

What had she been thinking, to accuse Lucas of only making love to her because she would eventually be wealthy? She'd let her suspicions get the better of her because deep down, she knew he wasn't the one responsible for what was happening to her. He couldn't have kissed her with such passion, on two occasions now, unless he genuinely felt something for her. So why would he be trying to drive her away — even if he did view Rafe as some sort of father figure and so felt a loyalty to him? As it was, she'd probably destroyed those feelings; killed any hope of a relationship with him. But worst of all, she missed him and found herself looking for him, listening for him, wherever she was.

And all of a sudden, the truth was staring her in the face. She was in love with him. She buried her face in her hands. What was she going to do? She'd almost certainly ruined everything with her wild accusations.

She needed something — someone — to distract her from all that was happening; someone to whom she could talk freely and openly. And there was really only one person she could call: Saffie. The friend she'd always turned to, confided in; who, no matter how troubled Christie felt, how desperate, could always make her feel better.

Saffie had been there for her every step of the way, from the age of nine or so. It had been Saffie who'd seen her through her father's illness and death, then her mother's. She'd been there in the aftermath, when Christie had felt so alone. So it stood to reason that she'd be there for her now, come what may.

There was no question in Christie's mind about that.

She pressed the number for her friend's mobile phone. It was answered almost at once.

'Saffie?'

'Who else would it be?' Saffie quipped. 'It's my phone.'

The sound of her friend's cheery voice brought the tears that never seemed far away at the present time springing into Christie's eyes. 'Saffie, how do you fancy a short holiday?'

'How does a dog fancy a beef dinner? Stupid question!' her friend predictably replied. 'Not that I'm calling myself a dog, you understand. That wretched Janey Morrison has already done that for me.'

'What?' Christie gasped.

'Yeah, the . . . well, I won't tell you what I called her. It's not fit for your ears. Just 'cause her boyfriend made a play for me. Can I help it if he fancies me? But to then describe me as a dog to all her friends — ' Saffie literally huffed. ' — when she has a face that could easily be mistaken for a squashed frog! Flippin' cheek.'

Christie couldn't speak for several moments for laughing. 'Oh, Saffie, I can always rely on you to cheer me up.'

'Anyway, to get back to the original question, yeah, course I fancy a holiday. Short or otherwise. Especially as I'm between jobs at the moment.'

'What? What happened?'

'Got the sack. Well, as they put it, business is bad and they need to shed staff. So that was me out. I did get a redundancy package so I'm not quite on my uppers yet, although I would have expected them to be a bit more generous.'

The shock of her friend's news drove Christie's troubles from her mind — temporarily, at any rate. It also rendered her speechless.

'Hello, still there?' Saffie asked.

'Oh. Yeah.'

'So to put it bluntly, I'd love a holiday. Has to be cheap, though, because I really need to hang on to every penny

I've got at the moment in case another job isn't immediately forthcoming.'

'No problem; you can stay here. Won't cost you a penny. I'm sure Grandmother won't mind.' She crossed her fingers and sent a mute prayer that she wouldn't be proved wrong. 'And . . . um, well, to be honest I need a friend at the moment.'

Saffie, running true to form, instantly picked up on the tremor that laced Christie's words. 'Why? What's happened? Are you okay?'

'I'll tell you all about it when you get here.'

'Wow! Too hot a topic for the phone then, huh?' Saffie said.

'You could say that. You never know who's around, listening.'

'Wow, a mystery! Great — just what I need to take my mind off my troubles. I've always fancied myself as a modern-day Miss Marple. I must remember to bring my knitting. Now, where did I put it?'

'Stop it,' Christie gasped, yet again

helpless with laughter. 'Look, just to be safe, I'll ask Grandmother if you can stay and I'll ring you right back.'

★   ★   ★

Venetia, of course, agreed straight away to Christie's request. 'We'd love to see your friend, Christie; she can have the room next to yours. I'll get Delia to prepare it immediately.'

So that was what happened and, within twenty-four hours, Saffie's blue Polo was pulling up in front of the house. Christie ran out, her relief and sheer happiness at seeing her friend bringing her yet again to the brink of tears.

'Well, thank God for the sat nav,' Saffie cried, even before she'd said hello. 'Heaven knows where I'd have ended up otherwise. Talk about the back of beyond.' Her glance riveted itself to the house. 'You didn't tell me you'd wandered into the realm of fairy-tales. Would you look at this place?' Her eyes were saucers as she took it all in. 'Sleeping

Beauty's not in there somewhere, is she? Because if she is, we're going to need a handsome prince. Or is he already in there? Please tell me he is.'

'Christie,' Venetia was standing in the doorway, 'and this must be — Saffie, is it?'

Saffie moved forward, her one hand extended towards the elderly woman, the other hanging on to a weighty-looking suitcase. 'This is so-o good of you.'

'Any friend of my granddaughter's is extremely welcome. Now, I have a tray of tea all ready, if you'd both like some. Leave your case in the hallway. Matt will take it to your room for you. I'm sure you must be parched after that long drive . . . um, Saffie.'

The two women followed the old woman into the house and on to the library. A muted 'Wow!' told Christie that her friend was suitably impressed by her grand surroundings. 'When's the butler going to show?' she softly asked.

'Ssh,' Christie hushed her. 'There is no butler.'

Once they were seated with cups of tea and homemade scones lavishly spread with strawberry jam and thick Devonshire clotted cream, Venetia embarked upon her customary inquisition, just as she'd done with Toby, until Christie decided enough was enough and said, 'If you don't mind, Grandmother, I'll show Saffie her room and then give her a tour of the house and gardens. I expect she'd like the chance to freshen up and unpack.' She raised a quizzical brow at her friend, at which point Saffie nodded — a bit too eagerly for Christie's peace of mind. She hoped her grandmother hadn't noticed.

'Of course, and I expect you girls will want to chat and catch up on each other's news.' She smiled understandingly. 'Dinner will be at six, so I'll see you then.'

But things didn't work out quite as Christie had expected. The two of them had barely reached the foot of the stairs when a voice spoke from behind them. It was Lucas. Christie hadn't heard the front door either opening or closing, so she was startled.

'I see we have another visitor,' he said. 'Won't you introduce me, Christie?'

Saffie's eyes widened once again to saucers. 'And here's the handsome prince, I do declare,' she murmured beneath her breath.

'Lucas,' Christie said, somewhat uneasily as she recalled their last encounter. 'Yes, my friend, Saffie; she's staying for a few days.'

Lucas strode forward, smiling warmly, one hand outstretched, the very epitome of charm. 'How very nice to meet you, um, Saffie. That's an unusual name.'

'Yes, my mother had a brainstorm when it came to naming me. The full name is Saffron. I prefer Saffie.'

Lucas positively grinned at her now. 'Ye-es, I can see why.' Throughout all of this, he hadn't as much as glanced at Christie. Now he did and she was forced to watch as his eyes cooled dramatically. 'And how are you, Christie? I don't seem to have seen much of you. Not avoiding me, are you?' His smile as he said this practically crackled with ice. Not that she was sure whether such a slight movement of the lips could be described as a smile, in any case.

'I could ask you the same question, Lucas,' she smartly retaliated.

'My explanation is perfectly simple. I've had a great deal of business to conduct, most of which has kept me out of the house.'

'Which would explain why you haven't seen much of me.' And now it was Christie's turn to smile, which she did with saccharine sweetness, a pointed contrast to his somewhat pathetic effort. Nonetheless, his coolness had provoked a piercing of anguish within her.

'Touché,' he softly said. 'Well, I trust I will see you both at dinner.'

'Oh, you will, you can be sure of that,' Saffie said. And to Christie's intense annoyance, she began to almost simper at him.

'Good. Well, I'll look forward to that.' He took the stairs two at a time and was gone before either of them could as much as blink an eyelid.

'You didn't tell me he was that gorgeous. A genuine prince. He can kiss me awake any time he wants,' Saffie murmured.

Christie didn't answer, chiefly because of the pain she was experiencing at the mere thought of Lucas kissing Saffie.

'So-o, do you think he fancies me?' Saffie eagerly asked. 'He looked as if that could be a distinct possibility.'

'How would I know?' Christie realized she sounded irritated, but she couldn't help it.

'Ooh, tetchy! So, what's wrong? Something's obviously troubling you; something serious if you couldn't tell me on the phone.'

'I'll tell you when you've freshened up, and believe me there's loads to tell.'

* * *

As avid curiosity was the main part of Saffie's personality, she wasted no time over her toilette. She was so quick, in fact, that Christie was still reapplying her own make-up when she walked into Christie's room.

'Here are the paints and things you asked me to get, Christie. Did you forget to bring any with you? Not like you. You usually bring more painting materials than clothes.'

That was Christie's cue to tell her friend what had been happening. She told her everything, except for the lovemaking between her and Lucas. It was too sensitive a subject for casual discussion.

'My God! No wonder you need a friend with you. But you can't seriously believe Lucas might be behind it all. I mean, he just seems too nice.'

'Nice isn't quite the adjective I'd have chosen,' Christie drily riposted.

'What then? Good-looking? Sexy? Rich?' she concluded on a hopeful note. 'I could sure do with a wealthy man at the moment . . . '

Christie shrugged. 'We-ell, he says

he's rich.' She hadn't mentioned her accusation of gold-digging on his part. She still broke into a sweat just thinking about it.

'But why would he want to drive you away? Rafe — yes, I can see why he would.'

'I did initially wonder if Lucas had been hoping to eventually inherit from Rafe. Rafe does seem to regard him as a son, so it would seem the natural thing to do, in which case wouldn't he want Rafe to end up with all the wealth? And if he could get Grandmother to disinherit me, which she might well do if I up and leave for no good reason, as far as she could see, it would all revert to Rafe. And I only have Lucas's word that he's wealthy in his own right.' At that juncture, she wasn't sure who she was trying to convince, her friend or herself. 'I don't know what to think, if you want the truth. The more I get to know him, the more I think he doesn't seem the type.'

'Well, my money's definitely on Rafe,'

Saffie put in. 'If he'd go as far as setting his dog on you, then he's positively dangerous. Have you told your grandmother about it all?'

Christie shook her head. 'I have no proof it's Rafe who's responsible, other than his wretched dog's antics, of course, and I'm loath to worry her; she has just lost her husband, after all.'

'Mmm, I can see your point.' She eyed Christie keenly. 'Uh — changing the subject, does Lucas have a girlfriend?'

'Well, I did see him one evening — it was while Toby was here — with a very glamorous woman. Figure to die for; silky smooth blonde hair — the sort that looks as if it's been ironed; long, long legs. You know the type. They look as if they should be up on the catwalk or on the big screen.'

'That's me out of the running then.' Saffie grimaced and glanced down over her own body: all five feet four and a half, and voluptuously proportioned.

'Well, he said he was just taking her

out to please her father, a business acquaintance of his, apparently.'

'So she's not a girlfriend as such?' Saffie sounded hopeful at that.

'He says not.'

'You've asked him then?'

Christie shrugged, preferring not to answer that for fear of incriminating herself.

Saffie eyed her once more. 'There's nothing going on between the two of you, is there? I won't be treading on your toes?'

Christie shook her head. She wasn't about to tell Saffie the truth about her feelings for Lucas, best friend or not. Saffie could at times be wildly indiscreet.

* * *

Dinner that evening passed off uneventfully for once, with none of the strife that invariably erupted whenever Venetia and Rafe were in the same room for any length of time. Victor's death looked to have subdued Venetia and made her less critical. Or maybe it was Saffie's presence that rendered things more amicable. Certainly her light-hearted banter kept everyone amused. Even Rafe managed a chuckle or two, which, as far as Christie was concerned, was unseen before this.

As for Lucas he didn't say very much at all, but his gaze lingered rather too frequently, Christie noted with a sinking heart, upon her lively, vivacious friend. Saffie, being Saffie, naturally also noticed this and began to play up to him quite outrageously.

'So what do you do for fun in these parts?' she eventually asked him. 'Because I want to join in.'

Lucas grinned and his eyes warmed as Saffie unabashedly flirted with him. 'Would you like me to show you one evening?'

'Yes, please.' She clapped her two hands together in a deliberately girlish way, looking up at him from beneath her lowered eyelids in a coquettish fashion. 'Are there many fleshpots around here? And, if so, where are they?'

Lucas openly laughed at that, but Christie saw her grandmother's expression stiffen, which didn't bode well for the rest of Saffie's stay. *Oh please, Saffie,* she mutely pleaded, *don't spoil things. Don't overdo the flirting.* Because Venetia clearly hadn't given up on her hopes for a match between her granddaughter and Lucas, and Christie wasn't sure how far she'd go in her drive to promote it. Send Saffie packing, maybe?

'Naturally I meant both of you,' Lucas smoothly said, slanting a glance that had assumed the properties of an iceberg towards Christie. He couldn't have made his preference for Saffie's company any more explicit. It also signified he had no intention of forgiving her any time soon for her hot-headed insinuations.

12

It was the following evening, with dinner over, that Saffie said, 'How about going out for an hour or two? The atmosphere here is a bit — what's the word? Oh yeah — dull, even taking into account the presence of the gorgeous Lucas.'

Christie could only be thankful that there was no one left to overhear her friend's candid remarks. Lucas had left the table as soon as the meal was over, declaring he had someone to see and must be going, which meant that as far as Saffie was concerned, the main attraction was gone. Venetia, Rafe and Alice wasted no time in following him, presumably heading for their respective bedrooms, which meant the two younger women were left alone at the table.

'Don't get me wrong,' Saffie went on, 'I love your grandmother and your aunt is a sweetie. Not sure about Uncle Rafe, though. Likes his vino a bit too much, eh? And my money's still on him for what's going on. He has the strongest motive, after all.'

'Yes, I know.'

'And it does let Lucas off the hook. Anyway,' Saffie went on, 'about tonight.'

'We could go and find a pub — hopefully, somewhere with something going on. There must be one even around here. Maybe we should head for Plymouth and, as you put it,' Christie added, her tone one of irony, 'the fleshpots.'

So that was what they did. They took Christie's car, as she wasn't in the mood to drink, and after much driving around managed to park, from where they walked until they found a place that had music coming from inside, as well as the sound of many voices. It also looked a bit more upmarket than the average pub.

'This'll do,' said Saffie, and without waiting for Christie to either agree or disagree dived through the entrance

273

and made a beeline for the bar.

Christie followed more cautiously, peering through the dimly lit interior, trying to pinpoint where her friend had gone. She quickly located her. Saffie was already standing in the centre of a group of young men. How did she do that — get men to gravitate spontaneously to her? It invariably happened. It must have something to do with her bubbly personality. Oh yeah, and an incredibly sexy figure, which was on full display tonight with a dangerously low-cut top and a pair of figure-hugging trousers. Her notion of appropriate wear for an evening out on the town.

Christie, on the other hand, was more conventionally dressed in linen trousers and a distinctly demure blouse. She belatedly wished she'd cast modesty aside and donned something a bit more daring, a bit more eye-catching. As it was, she felt — and suspected looked — like Saffie's older maiden aunt. Her only excuse was the limited amount of clothes she'd brought to

Devon with her, not expecting a wild night out.

'Christie, over here.' Saffie waved a glass of wine at her friend. 'Have a drink.'

A fair-haired man instantly handed Christie a glass of something or other — they must have a bottle of the stuff. 'Thanks,' she said, taking a cautious sip. One couldn't be too careful nowadays about accepting drinks from strangers. She'd read all sorts of horror stories about a date-rape drug. Still, it tasted okay. She was about to take another, larger mouthful when a hand shot out and whipped the glass from her.

'What the hell are you doing?' a rasping voice demanded to know. 'Do you know these men?'

Christie swivelled her head to see who it was talking in such a manner to her and found herself gazing straight into Lucas's blazing eyes. What on earth was he doing here? And what business was it of his what she was doing? 'I do now,' she snapped.

'Do you even know their names?'

'Not yet, but give me time.'

'They could be anyone.' Without as much as a blink, he whipped both her and Saffie's glasses from their hands and replaced them on the bar.

'Hey, hang on, mate, what the hell — ?' one of the men started to protest. Lucas ignored him.

'Wh-what?' Saffie gasped. 'Wh-what are you doing?' Her words were ever so slightly slurred as she peered through the gloom, trying to see who it was who had had the nerve to snatch her glass from her. She'd already had two or even three glasses of wine with her dinner, Christie knew — although she hadn't actually counted them — so she was well on her way to being more than a little intoxicated. 'Oh my,' she now sighed, 'the handsome prince has come to my rescue. How absolutely di-ivine,' she gushed, swaying dangerously. 'Sorry, chaps,' she said, grinning at the young men around her, 'have to go. You've been outgunned.'

Lucas took hold of her arm, snapping over his shoulder to Christie. 'Follow me.'

Well, if that wasn't just typical, decided Christie. No 'Please, would you follow me,' oh no. A simple, snapped 'Follow me,' and that was it. How could she be in love with such an arrogant man? Maybe she should snap back, 'No.' What would he do then? Throw her over his shoulder? She had a strong suspicion he might do just that. Nonetheless, as he was already leading Saffie away, Christie had no option but to follow. Although what he had made of Saffie's reference to him as the handsome prince, she didn't dare consider.

He led them to a table on the opposite side of the bar to where they'd been standing. How could he possibly have distinguished them in this gloom from here? Another man was sitting at the table, a delighted grin wreathing his face as he watched them approach. He got to his feet. 'Well, well, Lucas, what have you found? Not that I'm complaining.'

'Meet Saffie. Oh, and Christie.' He indicated Christie, lagging behind. She was beginning to feel like an afterthought in more ways than one. Could she have been wrong in her assumption that he must have feelings for her to make such passionate love to her? Could he, after all, only be after her eventual inheritance? Although someone should tell him that this wasn't the way to go about things, treating her like an afterthought.

'This is Nick Hallam, a good friend as well as a business associate.'

'Hi, Nick.' Saffie lurched forward, her hand outstretched. 'Great to meet you. Any friend of Lucas and all that.'

'Sit down, Saffie,' Lucas commanded, the words 'before you fall down' left silently suspended in the air.

'Sure will.' Saffie plumped herself down immediately opposite to Nick — an even more widely grinning Nick as his gaze lingered on the curvaceous display in front of him. Lucas took the seat at her side, leaving the one right opposite him for Christie.

'You're Mrs Wakeham's unknown granddaughter,' Nick turned to her and said. 'I've heard all about you.'

'Really?' So Lucas must have been talking about her. She slanted a sideways glance across the table at him, wondering what he'd said. Repeated her accusation of gold-digging? She doubted it.

However, her expression must have given her away, because Nick immediately said, 'Oh, all good things, I can assure you.'

She raised an eyebrow, at the same time directing another glance towards Lucas. But he looked totally enraptured by whatever it was Saffie was saying and wasn't listening.

'And you're every bit as lovely as he described.'

Lucas had said she was lovely? Her heartbeat quickened, as for the third time in as many minutes she again glanced his way.

Lucas, however, remained oblivious to all of this, and was asking Saffie, 'What would you like to drink?' He and Nick had glasses of beer in front of them.

'Wine, please,' Saffie promptly said.

'Christie?' he asked, again apparently as an afterthought.

'I'll have mineral water; I'm driving,' Christie put in. God, did she have to sound boring as well as look it? No wonder he preferred Saffie. She looked gorgeous and was heaps more fun to be with. And what was more, she wouldn't be calling his integrity into question.

Lucas signalled to a nearby barman to bring them some glasses, as well as a bottle of wine and some mineral water, which the man instantly did. Christie was grudgingly impressed. In a bar as crowded as this one was, such prompt service could only be classified as a miracle. Or did the waiter already know him and so awarded him special treatment? Mind you, Lucas's brand of arrogance would probably command instant compliance wherever he went. Just look how she and Saffie had unquestioningly obeyed him — well, Saffie had. She herself had dragged her feet a bit.

Lucas poured them both a glass of water, as well as a glass of wine for Saffie. Christie eyed her friend. Saffie could get a little impetuous — boldly so, after a few drinks. She'd seen her go and sit on a complete stranger's knee before now. She fervently hoped she wouldn't try the same thing with either Lucas or his friend, Nick. Although seeing how readily Lucas was responding to Saffie, maybe he'd welcome it. And she didn't think Nick would offer much in the way of complaint either.

However, Saffie restricted herself to chatting both men up. They didn't seem to mind this, although Nick's glance kept straying sideways to Christie. It provided some comfort to Christie to know that one man at least seemed to prefer her to the more lively Saffie. Eventually, Saffie got the message that it was Christie and not her that Nick was interested in and concentrated upon a spirited flirtation with Lucas.

'So tell me a bit about yourself,' Nick invited. 'I have to say, your story sounds fascinating; intriguing, even. A long-lost granddaughter turning up out of the blue.'

'Well I wasn't exactly lost, more completely unknown. I think my arrival came as a not altogether happy surprise to certain members of the family.' She was careful not to look at Lucas as she said this. She felt his gaze rest upon her, however. So despite Saffie's spirited and non-stop banter, he'd evidently heard every word.

'Oh, surely not.' Nick looked startled by this revelation.

She took a large gulp of her water, belatedly wishing it were wine. It might have given her the courage to say a bit more than, 'Yeah, afraid so. I don't mean my grandparents. After the initial shock they were pleased about it, but . . . ' She hesitated before thinking oh blow it, why shouldn't she say something? 'My uncle was . . . well, shall we say, less than thrilled.'

Nick studied her thoughtfully. 'I see. So are you going to be staying here? You live further north, don't you?'

'Yes, Worcestershire. But no, I don't think I'll be staying for much longer. I do have my own life to lead and a business to get up and running.'

'Christie is going to open an art gallery,' Lucas chipped in. So, as she'd suspected, he had been listening. 'She's a painter herself.'

'Wow! Beautiful and an artist. You'll do a self-portrait, naturally. I might even buy it — ' Nick smiled warmly, his eyes twinkling at her over the rim of his glass. ' — to remind me of you once you've gone. Of course, if you give me your phone number, I can ring you. That would be even better. I occasionally come to your part of the world, but even if I didn't — ' He smiled again. ' — I would certainly make a point of it now.'

Christie couldn't help responding. It had been ages since she'd enjoyed a harmless flirtation. It made a refreshing change. 'I'd love to see you.'

'Christie already has a . . . friend,' Lucas curtly interrupted.

Christie looked at him in surprise. He met her look almost challengingly. His eyes had darkened and his jaw hardened. He clearly wasn't best pleased with Nick and Christie's flirtation.

'Toby,' he went on. 'He also visited us a while back.'

'Oh, Toby's toast,' Saffie slurred. She'd been steadily downing her wine, Christie realized too late. 'Finished.' She slashed a finger across her throat. 'Gone. So Nick, ol' fella, the way's open for you.'

Lucas's gaze continued to laser Christie from the other side of the table. 'Is that right, Christie?'

Christie nodded, at the same time directing a baleful stare at her friend. She was surprised by Lucas's question. She'd believed he'd realized that the row he'd witnessed in the restaurant had been the end of her and Toby's relationship.

'How come? You seemed so . . . close, if the little scene which I interrupted was anything to go by.'

He must be referring to the kiss that he'd seen her and Toby share upon Toby's arrival; he couldn't mean the blazing row he'd been witness to in the restaurant. That would surely have suggested the exact opposite.

'It didn't seem fair to keep him hanging on, when . . . when . . . ' Her words petered out.

'Yes, when — ?'

Why was Lucas so interested, when he clearly preferred Saffie's company to hers? He made no secret of that.

'I don't return his feelings.' There, she'd said it.

'So is that what you were doing in the restaurant — ending things?' There was an intent look to him now as he awaited her answer.

Christie nodded.

'Great!' Nick exclaimed. 'That means there's a chance for me.'

'Oh, I wouldn't bet on that, Nick,' Lucas smoothly contradicted. 'I'm sure Christie will soon have a queue of suitors only too eager to replace poor Toby. She'll be a considerable heiress one day in the not-too-distant future, and with — '

'All men aren't like you, Lucas,' she snapped, cutting him off mid-sentence. Rude, she knew, but she was genuinely hurt that he'd say such things in front of others.

'Well, I for one would take Christie, with or without money,' Nick quietly put in.

'I'm sure you would,' Lucas muttered.

'Lucas obviously thinks that men will only want me for my money.'

'No, that's not what I think,' Lucas bit out. 'I was about to point out that with considerable wealth as well as good looks, you would have to be careful that you aren't taken advantage of. That's all.'

'Well, that's not what it sounded like, but thank you for your concern, Lucas.

However, I'm a big girl now, so I think — no, I know I can take care of myself.'

'Hey.' Saffie decided she'd been ignored long enough. 'I'm still here, you know. Would somebody mind passing me the wine? I'm running on empty.'

'No time.' Christie got to her feet. 'We have to go. I'm sure we've more than outstayed our welcome.'

'No such thing.' Nick stood too and placed an arm around her shoulders, trying to push her down into her seat again. 'We've only just begun.'

But Christie managed to stay upright. 'Nick, as nice as it's been to meet you, we really do have to go. I think Saffie needs her bed.'

'No, I don't — I need someone else's.' She drunkenly giggled before looking at Christie and grumbling, 'You can be such a spoilsport.' She glanced at both men. 'She can be such a prude.'

'Well, will I see you again before you go home?' Nick quietly asked Christie.

'I don't know. It depends what my grandmother has got planned.'

'Okay, so give me your phone number.' He stood up, pulling his mobile phone from his pocket to enter the number that Christie readily gave him. She steadfastly disregarded Lucas's frown of displeasure. Served him right. He shouldn't have implied that any admirers she might have in the future would only be interested in her for her money; shouldn't, in fact, judge others by his own standards. Not that she intended to see Nick again, but Lucas wasn't to know that. Let him wonder.

'Saffie,' she spoke impatiently now, 'come on, do.'

'Oh, okay,' her friend grumbled, 'party-pooper. She's always been the same,' she whispered confidentially to the two men. 'Bossy.' She swayed as she stood up, on the verge of falling over but for Lucas's hand shooting out to support her.

'Ta, Lucas,' She leant over to drop a kiss on his cheek. 'Mmm, you smell gorgeous. You don't fancy a quick snog, do you?'

Lucas gave a snort of laughter, but

unbent enough to return her kiss. 'A good night's sleep and you'll be a different person in the morning.'

'I don't want to be a different person,' she riposted. 'I'm quite happy to be me.' She grinned mischievously at him before sighing and saying, 'My prince.'

With that, he gave up any attempt to remain serious and gave a shout of laughter. 'That's a first. I've never been described as someone's prince before.' He dropped a kiss, this time onto her lips.

'Oh well,' Nick said, 'if everyone's having a snog, I may as well join in.' And he grabbed hold of Christie, pulling her into his arms, to capture her parted lips and kiss her with lengthy and enthusiastic ardour. Which would have been enjoyable but for the prickling sensation of Lucas's gaze boring into the back of her head. This annoyed her so much that out of sheer devilment, she wound her arms up and around Nick's neck, pressing herself wantonly against him.

'Okay,' he suddenly whispered against her mouth, 'let's not overdo it. Lucas is already fit to murder me; any more and he'll definitely do it.'

She pulled back. Mirth twinkled at her from his blue eyes. He knew exactly what she was up to. She grinned back ruefully, even a touch regretfully. He was such a nice man, just not the man for her.

'Go for it, gal,' he murmured. 'You're just what he needs.' He spoke directly into her ear now, giving the impression that he was whispering sweet nothings.

She couldn't stop herself from slanting a glance at Lucas. His jaw was clenched, a single muscle flexing on one side of it, his expression thunderous as he watched her and Nick. She didn't know what to think. One minute he seemed to have only contempt for her, the next he was displaying unmistakable jealousy.

Of course, Saffie started moaning the moment they were outside the bar, 'Did you have to spoil my fun? I was in there with Lucas, and you wouldn't even let him come out with us. He'd probably have driven me back,' she said with a sigh. Lucas had wanted to escort them to the car, but Christie had refused, insisting there was no need. 'We're parked only minutes away in a well lit street.'

With visible reluctance, he had let them go. So it was unfortunate that they were only halfway back to the car when a group of youths appeared from nowhere, whistling and calling, 'Come on, darlin'. Wanna a good time?' One was already reaching out for Christie when there was a shout and Lucas hurled himself between her and the stranger. He pushed Christie and Saffie behind him just as Nick ran towards them all.

'Clear off, lads,' Lucas then calmly told the group. 'They're with us.'

'Okay, man,' the ringleader said. 'Enough said.' They sauntered off with good-tempered waves.

Lucas turned accusingly to Christie.

'That's exactly what I was worried about. Now, will you please let us walk you to your car?'

Well and truly chastened by the thought of what could have happened if Lucas hadn't intervened, Christie simply nodded and said, 'The car's just around this corner.'

And in truth, she was glad of their help in getting Saffie back, because belatedly the alcohol was having its full effect. She could barely put one foot in front of the other. It took both men to support her for the short distance to the car and then get her inside.

'Do you want me to drive you?' Lucas asked. 'I can collect my car tomorrow.'

'No, really. Thank you, but we'll be fine. And I've only been drinking water.'

'Okay, but I'll follow you. You'll need help the other end, I suspect.'

He was right, she did. Eventually, between them, they got Saffie into the house and up to her bedroom.

'Thank you, Lucas,' Christie finally said. 'I'll take it from here.'

She was sure Saffie would need help undressing and wouldn't welcome assistance from Lucas, handsome prince or no.

'Sure? I could call your grandmother, or even Delia.'

'God, no.' She dreaded to think what either of the two older women would make of Saffie's condition. 'I'll manage on my own, really,' she added in response to his anxious look.

⋆   ⋆   ⋆

The next morning Saffie didn't appear until midday, and even then her face was the colour of undercooked rice pudding.

'Oh, my Lord,' she groaned. 'How much wine did I have to drink last night?'

'Too much, clearly,' Christie quipped.

'It doesn't usually affect me so badly.' She eyed Christie. 'Did I make a complete fool of myself?'

'You mean other than telling Lucas that he was your prince?'

Saffie groaned and hid her face in her hands. 'Oh no, I didn't, did I?' She peeked nervously through her fingers at her grinning friend. 'How on earth am I going to face him?'

'You might not have to. Grandmother told me he's away on business for a few days.'

Which had been a major disappointment to Christie. She'd wanted to see him to try and gauge how accurately she'd interpreted his reactions to her and Nick's kiss, and she couldn't do that without him being here. Maybe he'd decided he'd revealed too much of his feelings, so he'd grabbed the excuse of a business trip to make his escape and give them both a breathing space. She didn't know whether to be relieved or not.

After that, Saffie and Christie spent a few days driving out and sightseeing. Rafe, too, kept out of the way, so that some evenings it was just Venetia and Alice eating with them. It made for a peaceful, relaxed time and Christie felt that she got to know her grandmother and great-aunt a good deal better.

The time came, of course, when Saffie had to leave. 'I need to get home and find myself a job. When are you coming back?' she asked Christie. 'Or are you intending to stay here?'

'I don't know,' Christie sighed. 'I love being here, and now that all the things that have been happening seem to have stopped . . . Well, I just don't know. I'll ring you and let you know.'

A sense of apprehension and deep misgiving had overtaken her with the imminent prospect of Saffie leaving. She wondered, even as she spoke, whether the time of uninterrupted tranquillity had been simply because Saffie had been here with her. So did that mean it would all start up again once she'd gone? Christie didn't know if she would be able to bear it if it did. Maybe it would, in the long run, be best to leave, and remove the threat of her presence to whoever it was. Rafe, she was becoming increasingly convinced. Yet, wouldn't that be conceding defeat? Something she had always hated doing.

But as she stood, waving Saffie off, her fears intensified, and it was all she could do not to run after her friend and plead with her to stay.

She didn't, of course. Instead she told herself not to be so silly; so pathetic. So a few paints and sketches had been ruined. She herself hadn't been threatened in any way. Well, that wasn't strictly true; she'd definitely felt threatened by Samson.

Once the small car had disappeared down the winding driveway, she went back into the house. She'd do some painting in oils for a change. The day was a fine one, and it would take her mind off Saffie's departure. Her friend had brought her more painting materials, in particular a couple of canvases; they wouldn't be so easy to destroy. But just to be sure of that, she'd store the completed work somewhere safe; somewhere where no one would find it. Somewhere like the top of the wardrobe.

She fetched her things from her bedroom and returned to the garden. The conditions were perfect. The air was crystal-clear, so much so that she could see the most minuscule details of everything she wished to capture on canvas. As she set up her portable easel by the side of the lake, a couple of mallards flew in and landed with consummate skill on the water just a few feet away. And then, just to complete the idyllic scene, a family of moorhens serenely paddled out from amongst the reeds that fringed the water.

With everything ready, she perched on her folding stool and picked up her palette, already laid out with her choice of oil paints, and several brushes. She'd managed to outline the shapes of the ducks and one of the moorhens when she was unexpectedly joined by her aunt Alice. The old lady, with some commotion, settled herself onto the grass by the side of Christie. She'd even brought a cushion for that very purpose, presumably. By the time Christie looked back again, both the ducks and all but one of the moorhens had vanished. She only just managed to suppress her sigh of disappointment. Not that she didn't welcome her aunt's company; she did. She just wished she hadn't made sufficient noise to scare all the wildlife away.

'Your mother loved to paint in watercolours, you know. I never saw her use oils. I see that you do.'

Christie was surprised. She hadn't known her mother painted. 'Did she?'

'Oh, yes. I used to sit alongside her sometimes too. I was very fond of Laura. I understood, in a way, why she left.'

Christie said nothing, content to let Alice ramble on.

'And why it was with Adam,' she

went on. 'Adam was a much more considerate man than Rafe. But oh my, you should have seen Rafe in those days. So handsome. No wonder Laura fell for him.' She lapsed into reflective silence. Christie wondered if she was remembering the events of those long-ago days.

'I saw Jennifer Holby in the village a few days ago,' she said. 'She said that Rafe gambled; still gambles.'

'Did she? You mustn't take all that people tell you at face value.'

'Why not? It seemed pretty clear to me.'

'About Rafe . . . It wasn't — isn't — all Rafe's fault. Venetia hasn't been all that a mother should be. He consoles himself, perhaps not altogether wisely at times.'

A heron flew over, its harsh call filling the air. It looked as if it was about to land on the opposite side of the lake but changed its mind at the last moment and, with much flapping of its huge wings, flew on. Perhaps it had spotted the two people sitting across from it.

Alice froze, her face losing every vestige of colour. She grabbed Christie's arm. 'Did you see that? Did you?'

'Yes. Wasn't it beautiful?' She knew what her aunt was thinking and tried desperately to distract her. 'Do you think I should paint that tree, or will it stop the eye exploring further?'

'It means death,' Alice gasped. 'You saw one when you first arrived, didn't you? And Victor died. Oh dear, oh dear,' she whimpered. 'It's a sign.' She pulled at Christie's arm. 'Christie, I beg of you: leave. Leave now, please. Oh dear.' She stumbled to her feet. 'I must go. Rafe's calling. I can hear him.'

13

Christie sat stunned, watching the old woman practically run away. For someone in her late seventies, she was remarkably agile. And what had she meant? 'It's a sign. Leave now, please.' She'd sounded afraid. Did she know something that Christie didn't?

Despite the heat of the day, she shivered. It was true: her grandfather had died after the sighting of a heron. Could the same thing happen to her? Or to her aunt? Was that why she had sounded so panic-stricken? Not out of fear for Christie, but for herself?

Oh for heaven's sake — she was being ridiculous now. Things like that just didn't happen. The words were nothing more than the ramblings of an old woman. The beginnings of senility, maybe. Alice, at times, didn't seem to be of this world. Her eyes would cloud and she would appear to be somewhere else entirely.

She heard the sound of footsteps once more behind her. Lucas? He'd been gone for several days. He must have had a great deal of business to conduct. Or had he deliberately stayed away? Saffie had been torn between disappointment at not seeing him again, and relief that she didn't have to apologize for her behaviour the night they'd met in the pub. 'He didn't even keep his promise to take us out one evening,' she moaned. 'I must have put him off the idea with my drunken antics. He was most likely afraid I'd give a repeat performance,' she mournfully finished.

'I'm sure it wasn't that. He liked you.' Christie was half-hearted in her reassurance; her thoughts were on other matters. Mainly, her friend's imminent departure. 'Obviously he must have had some urgent business to deal with — something that simply wouldn't wait.'

'Maybe.' Saffie eyed her for a long, silent moment. 'Look, stop worrying. You are, aren't you? Worrying that once I've gone, things will start to happen again. I'm sure — no, I'm positive that it isn't Lucas. Look at the way he leapt to our defence that night. He wouldn't have done that, surely, if it was him. He'd have left us — you — to your fate. But he didn't. Gallantly, and careless of his own safety, he rode to our rescue. A true prince.' She sighed dramatically.

'Stop it,' Christie laughed helplessly. And now her heart leapt at the thought that it might be Lucas behind her and, eagerly, she turned to look.

But it was only Rafe. After an initial stab of the most intense disappointment she'd ever experienced, her pulse quickened and then raced madly. Her uncle was the last person she wanted to be alone with.

'Hello there,' he said.

Christie eyed him. He looked friendly enough. But she couldn't help recalling the way he'd tried to persuade the family that she had been the one to steal the brooch. And then there were the things he'd said to her; his sinister-sounding words about the dangers out on the moors. And last, but not least, there was his horrible dog. She still wondered whether he'd actively encouraged the wretched animal to terrify her. All of which led her to wonder, could Saffie be right that Lucas knew nothing about any of it, especially the destruction of her work? She so wanted to believe that.

'Hello. Did Aunt Alice find you?' She hoped her words would induce him to go and find Alice and thus leave her alone once more.

'No.' He looked puzzled. 'Was she looking for me?'

'She said she heard you calling her.'

'It wasn't me. I've been out; just got back. Thought I'd come and join you.' He proceeded to settle himself on the grass at her side — the very last thing she wanted, especially as she detected whisky on his breath. Still, at least he hadn't brought Samson with him, something she supposed she should be grateful for.

She edged her stool away from him. If he'd only just got back, how had he known she was out here? He couldn't have spotted her from the front of the house. He must have come looking for her. Why? It was then that Alice's warning blazed back at her. 'Leave now — please.'

Christie stared at Rafe. He couldn't be intending her harm, surely? Not out here in the open. Even as she had the thought, the sun disappeared behind a cloud and a shadow fell over them both. She gasped. A sign of what was to come? An omen? Oh, for goodness sake — she was becoming as fanciful as her great-aunt.

Then Rafe began to speak. 'This lake is very deep, you know. It was once a quarry. Said to be bottomless in places. Did you know that?' He laughed. It was a hollow sound; mirthless. 'Adam and I believed that implicitly when we were boys. We used to spend ages gazing into the depths. An old man had fallen in, apparently, many years before and completely disappeared. They never found his body. Adam and I hoped we'd see him floating to the surface. Used to lay bets on it, in fact.' He laughed again. 'Never did, of course.'

He looked away from her. Christie followed his gaze with her own. The surface of the water had turned grey in the absence of sunshine. She glanced up. Leaden thunderclouds were mounting, obliterating the last vestiges of blue. She shivered, even though it wasn't at all cold. Rather the opposite, in fact. The air was humid; positively clammy. Beads of sweat broke out on her brow.

'We used to say, Adam and I, if you want to dispose of something, chuck it in here.' He gave a bark of laughter. It made Christie jump. 'I did once.' She stared, horrified at him. 'Oh, it's okay; it wasn't a body, just my school report. I filled the envelope with small stones.

My parents never knew what happened to it. Didn't do me any good, of course. Mother simply asked the school to send another. I was grounded for weeks.'

Maybe she should ask him outright if he was the one behind what was happening to her. But if he wasn't and she wrongly accused him, he'd resent her even more.

And if she was right? What would he do then, knowing he'd been found out? Something even worse than tearing paintings and scribbling on the mirror?

Again she eyed the grey, forbidding water of the lake. Someone had already disappeared, his body never recovered. What if the same thing should happen to her? It wouldn't take much. A quick shove — Rafe was a big man, much bigger than her. She wouldn't be able to fight him. And the banks were quite steep. If she went in, there was a real risk that she wouldn't be able to clamber out again.

The fact was Rafe could do whatever he wanted. There was no one to see. A deep fear began to manifest itself within her, so it was with a tremendous sense of relief that Christie felt the first raindrops fall on her bare arms. 'It's raining. Come on, let's go in.'

But Rafe looked miles away.

Christie tried again. 'Uncle Rafe, come on.'

'You go.' He spoke absently. His gaze was still fixed on the lake. 'I'll follow in a minute.'

Thunder rolled ominously in the distance as Christie, needing no second bidding, packed up her painting equipment. The lake, which had seemed so picturesque a short time ago, looked dark and dangerous. She started to run towards the house as lightning forked overhead. She did glance back, just the once. Rafe was still sitting, motionless, staring down into the murky water.

A heron flew over, its call loud, harsh. Rafe still didn't move; didn't even look up at it. It was as if it didn't exist; as if the storm wasn't happening.

Christie was soaked through by the time she ran into the house. Her grandmother was in the hallway.

'My goodness, child, go and dry yourself this minute. You'll catch your death.'

Once in her room, Christie stripped off her dripping clothes. It wasn't until she went to the chest of drawers to find some dry things to put on that she saw the note. It was propped up against the bowl that sat on the top. The words had been cut from a newspaper. They said: Be warned — the money will never be yours. If you value your life, go away now.

She sank onto the bed, the paper crushed in her hand. This had to be Rafe's handiwork; there was no one else it could be. He must have come in while she'd been at the lake and left it here. His words concerning the depth of the lake and the missing man hadn't been just a warning; they'd been a threat.

There was only one consolation to be had and that was that she could now be one hundred percent sure it wasn't Lucas doing these things to her. He still hadn't returned.

She skipped dinner that night, preferring to remain in her room. She couldn't be sure that she wouldn't blurt out her accusations about Rafe, and without positive proof of the guilty party being him, she could find herself on very sticky ground indeed. Delia brought her a tray of chicken salad which, against all of her expectations, she ate.

She slept badly, though, mainly because she couldn't stop turning over and over in her mind all that had happened. Again, she'd told no one about the note. After all, how could she tell two elderly women that she believed she was being threatened by a close member of their family? A son to one, and a nephew to the other. She assumed that Rafe had eventually come in from the lakeside; she hadn't actually seen him. But she couldn't keep avoiding him by staying in her room. She didn't know what to do.

Maybe it was, after all, time to leave — to forget everything that had happened here? Forget the family . . . But how could she forget about her grandmother? She couldn't. She'd grown to love her deeply, and her leaving suddenly with no explanation would surely break the old woman's heart.

Eventually she did sleep, worn out with her deliberations, and didn't wake until the knock came on her door the next morning.

'Can I come in?' It was Delia.

'Yes, Delia.'

'I've brought you some breakfast. I thought, as you've slept late, you might not be feeling well. Mrs Wakeham told me about your soaking yesterday.'

Christie stared down at the bacon and eggs and felt the nausea rush up into her throat.

'So-sorry, I'm going to be sick,' she groaned as she made a dash for the bathroom.

Delia laid down the tray and followed her. 'I'll get your grandmother. You're clearly not at all well. You're as white as snow.'

* * *

Christie was still being violently sick when her grandmother bustled into the bathroom. She took one look at her ashen-faced granddaughter and said, 'Delia, go and call Doctor Brookes immediately.'

Christie felt too ill to argue with this and made no protest when the doctor arrived.

'I fear she's caught a chill, Doctor,' Venetia told him. 'She did get very wet yesterday.'

He eyed her pallid complexion as he took her temperature. 'I don't think it's a chill. A drop of rain wouldn't result in this — not in a healthy young woman.' He eyed Christie speculatively. 'What have you had to eat over the past forty-eight hours?'

'The same as everyone else,' Christie said weakly.

'No, Christie,' Venetia corrected her. 'You had chicken last night. We had steak and kidney. She doesn't care for offal of any sort,' she explained to the doctor.

'Hmmm, I'd say that's what it was then. A spot of food poisoning. Have to be careful with chicken at this time of the year.'

Venetia's lips tightened. 'I'll have a word with Delia.' There was a determined glitter to her eye now. Christie decided she wouldn't want to be in Delia's shoes.

'Rest and plenty to drink. Nothing to eat for twenty-four hours,' the doctor ordered. 'Should do the trick.'

Christie remained in bed for the rest of that day. She literally felt too ill to get up.

It was the next morning that Alice rushed into her room. Christie was startled; she was still in bed. 'My dear girl, I did try to warn you. The appearance of a heron means death. Oh dear me. You really should leave — must leave.' She pressed her lace hankie to her trembling lips.

Determined not to give any credence to Alice's preposterous theory, Christie tried to reassure her. She did look genuinely concerned. 'Aunt Alice, I'm not going to die. It was a touch of food poisoning. The chicken, we think. I'm feeling a lot better now.'

'Why won't she listen to me? Why?' Alice whispered, her wild-eyed gaze flitting round the room. 'She's been poisoned — oh dear, dear, dear . . . '

'Who are you talking to, Aunt Alice?' Christie asked, because she had seemed to be addressing someone. But Alice had gone. Christie was alone once more.

She frowned. Could her great-aunt be right to be so concerned? Could she have been poisoned deliberately? That was what her words had seemed to suggest. And if she was right, then events had taken a decided turn for the worse. Her life could be at risk.

But would Rafe — and who else could it be but Rafe? — really go to the lengths of murder to be rid of her?

★ ★ ★

Eventually, when Christie felt well enough to leave her bed and go downstairs, the first person she saw was Lucas. He came straight to her and lifted her chin with a finger, tilting her head to give him a better view of her face.

'Your grandmother told me you've been unwell. You're too pale, Christie. Beautiful, but too pale.' His gaze moved to her lips. He was going to kiss her. A blush warmed her skin, something that rarely happened. He smiled and looked back into her eyes. He knew what she'd been hoping for. 'I do love a woman who blushes. So rare these days.'

Although he hadn't kissed her, he was very definitely flirting with her. Her heart thudded tempestuously. It was as if all that had happened between them had been solely in her imagination. Her rejection of his lovemaking, her tacit accusation of him only wanting her for her eventual inheritance, his thunderous anger at her flirtation with Nick. Although he had seemed to unbend a little as he'd helped her with Saffie. Maybe his time away had helped him view things in a different light; put events into some sort of perspective? Or maybe it was simply that he'd missed her. Or could it be that Nick had said something to him? After all, he'd deduced pretty quickly the way Christie felt about Lucas. Maybe he'd relayed that to his friend. The questions came thick and fast. It was a pity that the answers didn't follow suit.

'Saffie said goodbye, by the way.'

'Oh dear, she's gone and I didn't get round to taking you both out.' He did look genuinely sorry.

'That doesn't matter. Um, is your business concluded?' she asked. 'Only, you've been gone some time.'

'Yes, and very satisfactorily. I've only just got back.' He paused fractionally. Then, with a lifted eyebrow, and in a voice that was throbbing with emotion, he huskily asked her, 'Have you missed me?'

For the first time then, she wondered whether he'd deliberately stayed away, hoping that she would indeed miss him. If so, his ploy had worked.

'Well, I suppose I did miss you — a little,' she concluded softly.

'Good,' he murmured as he gave her a long, lingering look before saying, 'Sadly, though, business calls once more.' Upon which note he disappeared through the front door, leaving Christie feeling totally bereft.

* * *

Next day she received another, even more explicit, warning. One that sent a chill all the way down her spine. It was scrawled in thick black ink across the mirror, in capital letters this time

— the intention, she guessed, to lend the words more impact.

It said, YOUR NEXT ILLNESS COULD BE YOUR LAST. LEAVE WHILE YOU STILL CAN.

14

Christie knew she couldn't keep this to herself any longer; couldn't ignore it now that her life had undeniably been threatened. So, without giving herself any time to reconsider, she sought out her grandmother. She told her everything. About the ripped-up paintings, the ruined paints, the spoilt clothes, the earlier writing on the mirror, the anonymous note with the words cut from a newspaper, the fact that she believed someone had planted the brooch amongst her things to try and discredit her in her grandmother's eyes, the menacing behaviour of Samson — at Rafe's behest, she was now convinced. And finally she led her to her bedroom and showed her the current writing on the mirror.

'Why haven't you told me about any of this before?' Venetia angrily demanded. The colour had leached from her face as Christie related all that had been happening.

'I didn't want to worry you.'

Venetia clicked her tongue in annoyance. 'Silly child. You should have told me straight away.'

'I think it's all down to Uncle Rafe — everything,' Christie went on. 'I think he even poisoned the chicken, just enough to make me sick, and then issued this warning that next time it will be much more serious.'

Venetia shook her head, her expression one of incredulous disbelief. 'I know Rafe can be rather stupid, but this? Never . . . '

'He resents me being here, Grandmother. He resents even more the fact that I'm a beneficiary in your will.'

'But that's a whole different thing to actually poisoning you. And with what?' Venetia's voice rose as shock consumed her.

'Rat poison? You must keep some in a house this size.'

'I'll speak to him. If it was him, I'll

get to the bottom of it, never fear. I give you my word on that.' A very steely and determined look had revived some of her natural skin tone. 'And if it wasn't him, I'll call the police.'

'Grandmother,' Christie called after her, 'I think it's time I left. It'll give everything and everyone a chance to settle down. I'll come back in a month or so.' That would also allow her and Lucas time to evaluate their true feelings — that was, providing she'd correctly read Lucas's behaviour upon their last meeting and it wasn't all just play-acting upon his part.

Oh God, she couldn't bear to think that. Her heart would break. She loved him so much.

'Let me speak to Rafe first,' her grandmother said, 'and then we'll decide what to do.'

* * *

Venetia must have gone immediately to confront Rafe, because when Christie

321

left her room, having packed the few belongings that she'd brought with her in case she did decide to leave, she heard the sound of Rafe's voice raised in outraged denial. She wasn't surprised. He was hardly going to admit to what had been happening to Christie.

'How dare you accuse me of such a thing?' Rafe was shouting. 'Poison? Where the blazes would I get such a thing? And writing anonymous letters? Destroying paintings? No way!'

'Well, who else would it be?' Venetia, in contrast to her son, sounded perfectly calm. 'You're the one with the grudge, Rafe, and the motive.' This was an astonishing turnaround from her defence, just moments ago, of Rafe.

'How dare you? You-you're mad. I would never do anything to hurt Christie. I might resent her arrival, and okay I admit I've teased her now and then, but I would never — *never* — lay a finger on her. What do you think I am, a monster?'

'Rafe!' Venetia's voice was suddenly

sharp with alarm.

Christie ran down the stairs and into the sitting room. Rafe and Venetia were standing close together in front of the fireplace, each glaring furiously at the other. Alice was sitting in a nearby chair, her face chalky with horror as she stared at the other two people, her hankie for once lying discarded on her lap.

'It was me,' she burst out. 'I did it. All of it.' She promptly covered her mouth with both hands, as if trying to stem any further incriminating words.

Venetia spun to stare incredulously at her sister. 'Don't be ridiculous, Alice. How could it have been you? You're taking the blame to protect Rafe, as usual.'

'No, Venetia, it was me. Truly.'

'But-but why?'

'Do you really need to ask? I couldn't bear to see Rafe lose out again. He's always come second-best to Adam. He even lost his wife to him. I couldn't bear to see him lose his rightful inheritance, too. He is my son, after all.' She again clapped a hand to her mouth.

For once, Venetia was lost for words. As was Christie. All she could do was stare, totally shocked by what the old lady was telling them all. It had been her scatty aunt who'd been responsible for everything. It was unbelievable. But what was equally unbelievable was that Rafe — Rafe was her son.

'What the hell are you talking about?' It was starkly evident that if Alice's statement was true, Rafe hadn't known.

Venetia did manage to speak now, albeit shakily. 'It's-it's true, Rafe. Alice is your mother.'

'B-but how?' Rafe was completely stunned. 'Do you mean — ' He staggered to a chair and slumped down into it. ' — I've been living a lie all these years? We've all been living a lie?'

Venetia nodded. Alice twittered, 'I'm sorry.'

'Why?' Rafe was speaking directly to Venetia now. 'Why would you let me think I'm your son?'

'Because Alice found herself pregnant at eighteen. A result of a brief fling with the local publican's son.'

'B-but your and Victor's names are on my birth certificate as my parents.'

'Yes,' Venetia said.

'Th-then how?'

'When Alice told me she was pregnant . . . well, she was terrified of what our parents would say; what everyone would say. She'd have been forced to give you up, have you adopted. Things were very different in those days. Our parents would never have accepted an illegitimate child. So, as I couldn't seem to conceive — Victor and I had been trying for two years . . . '

It was obvious to Christie that Venetia hated having to admit this — a personal failing in her view, clearly, 'Victor was desperate for a child, so I — we, Victor and I that is — decided that if Alice was agreeable — and she was — we would pretend it was me who was pregnant. Alice wore loose clothing and I . . . well, I padded myself out. It wasn't difficult.

'Anyway, for the final months, Victor, Alice and I went on a long trip, ending up in Edinburgh where Alice gave birth to you, Rafe. She gave her name as Venetia and I became Alice. It meant we could register you as my and Victor's son. So when we subsequently returned home we could tell everyone you were ours. Even our parents didn't know the truth.'

'I didn't love your father, Rafe,' Alice put in, tearfully, 'so I didn't tell him I was carrying his child. I-I always — ' She glanced nervously at her sister. ' — loved Victor.'

Venetia's expression darkened, but Christie suspected that Alice's words came as no great surprise.

'But-but Victor wasn't interested in me. It was only ever Venetia as far as he was concerned. I learned to be content with just seeing him every day.'

'I can't believe it,' Rafe gasped. He looked on the verge of complete collapse, in fact, in the wake of Venetia and Alice's revelations. 'And now, what have you been doing, Aunt Al — I mean, Mother?' He was clearly determined to get to the bottom of what was happening, despite the astonishing revelations that he'd just heard.

'I-I ripped up Christie's paintings,' Alice told him. 'Planted the brooch, spoilt her clothes and her paintings, wrote on the mirror, left an anonymous letter . . . ' She opened the small bag that she always carried with her and, from within, produced a piece of neatly folded newspaper. She opened it up and showed them the spaces where words had once been. 'I warned her to leave while she still could, but I didn't poison her. It was wicked of me, I know, but I took advantage of her bout of food poisoning to pile on the pressure for her to leave. I didn't think you'd blame Rafe, Christie.' Her pale eyes brimmed with tears.

'Oh, dear . . . I'm so sorry,' she continued. 'I've been a very silly old woman. I didn't stop to think things through. Of course you'd blame Rafe. Who else would you blame? So silly. But I didn't want to harm you,

Christie. I thought if I scared you badly enough, you'd leave and not return. Venetia would be so angry, so disappointed in you, that she'd disinherit you. I'm sorry; I've done every wicked thing. But you wouldn't go. Why wouldn't you go? None of this would have happened then.'

Someone else had entered the room — Lucas. From his stunned expression it was apparent that he'd heard most of this. He strode across to Christie and put his arm around her. 'Are you okay?' he gently asked. His eyes warmed as he gazed at her, the amber flecks she'd glimpsed several times now glittering in their depths.

How could she have ever thought it might be him? And Rafe — she'd been completely mistaken there too. She nodded.

'Well, it explains the way you've always treated me, Mother — or should I say, Aunt Venetia?' Rafe snorted. 'I'm not your son.'

'Not biologically, no. But Victor and I

always regarded you as our son right from the start. However, your behaviour over the years, Rafe, has frankly grieved me. Your gambling, your drinking, your lack of any profitable occupation. Adam didn't steal her; you drove Laura away. You were always a difficult boy, but I did try to do my best for you. And I can honestly say that both Victor and I did love you. I do still love you, although it might not always look that way. Everything I've done and said has only ever been in your best interest, to try and make you see that you're wasting your life.'

Some of the colour that had gradually drained away as he'd listened to the two women returned to Rafe's face at this admission. His eyes shone with what looked suspiciously like tears. 'Yes, well, I do need to take my share of the blame, and admit I haven't been the best of sons. And when I was a boy, you were always fair and even-handed between me and Adam.'

He turned to Christie then. 'This

is partly my fault. Well, all of it, in fact. If I hadn't been so angry towards you, so bitterly resentful, maybe Aunt Alice . . . ' He corrected himself again. 'Mother . . . wouldn't have resorted to such tactics. I'm truly sorry. None of this has been your fault. Can you forgive me? Can we start again?' He held out a hand to her. 'Now that I know the truth, well, in a funny sort of way it's helped. I really will try a bit harder and turn over a new leaf, especially with my only niece.' His brow wrinkled. 'Is that what you are? I'm not sure.'

'Oh, Uncle Rafe, it doesn't matter what I am.' Christie took his hand. The relief that flooded over her was truly overwhelming. 'Of course we can start again. I'll be your niece, your cousin — whatever. And, Aunt Alice — ' She swung to the old woman, who was by this time weeping softly into her handkerchief. ' — don't worry about anything. You love your son and just wanted the best for him. And you did try and persuade me to leave. If it hadn't been for my stubbornness . . . '

'Yes, well,' Venetia intervened, 'we must all make an effort from now on. We are family, after all — the only one any of us have.'

*   *   *

Eventually Christie managed to make her escape from the room, leaving Rafe and Alice — Rafe especially — to reconcile themselves to their new relationship. Which wouldn't take long, Christie guessed. Because once Rafe had recovered from his shock, he'd looked as if he positively welcomed the fact that Alice was his biological mother. At any rate, Alice had been weeping in his arms and Rafe had been murmuring, 'Sssh, Mother, it's all right. Everything's going to be all right. A new beginning, eh? For us all . . . '

Christie was yearning for the peace and quiet of her own bedroom. She needed to sort things out in her own mind. The impact of what she had been told was immense. All she could think was — she'd got the motive right; she'd just been blaming the wrong person. Mind you, as Rafe had admitted, he had invited the blame. If he'd behaved better . . .

'Christie.'

The single word halted her progress up the stairs. She swivelled. It was Lucas. He'd followed her.

'Where are you going?'

'Home. I've got an art gallery to open — or had you forgotten that?'

'No. But you're not going anywhere until I've had my say. Please come back down.'

Christie took a deep breath, trying not to mind his authoritative words and manner, and walked back down the stairs. 'Go on then.'

'The main thing I want to say is, I love you.'

Christie froze, her breath catching in her throat.

'You must have guessed, surely? Especially after the other night.' He smiled grimly. 'I could have murdered Nick — almost did. Only, he told me how he thought you felt about me — mainly in a last-ditch attempt to save his own skin, I suspect.' He smiled again — apprehensively, it had to be said.

Here was a side of Lucas — a diffidence — she'd never before glimpsed; a hugely endearing side. He'd always looked so sure of himself.

'Well, I hoped, I suppose . . . ' She wrinkled her brow. 'Why didn't you say something?'

'I wasn't at all sure you'd welcome a declaration of love from me. You didn't seem to welcome my kisses and you said some pretty harsh things. I've never before been called a gold-digger. Which was a little unjust, because I'm a fairly wealthy man in my own right. Anyway, I thought if I gave you some more time . . . '

'Oh, Lucas, I'm so sorry. If you knew how much I've regretted what I said . . . '

He gave a shaky grin. 'I just wish you'd told me all that was happening. I could have tried to help.' He stopped talking then and stared at her. Something stirred in the depths of his eyes. 'You thought it might have been me responsible for it all, didn't you? That's why I always felt there was something standing between us — a barrier of some sort. My God, Christie. You thought I would do all of that — to you?'

He did look genuinely shocked as the impact of it all finally hit him: that, and deeply hurt. So much so, that all Christie wanted in that second was to hold him in her arms and wipe that anguished expression away.

She didn't though. Instead, she tried to explain. 'No. We-ell, if I'm honest, I didn't know what to think. But my favoured candidate was always Rafe. I hoped and prayed it wasn't you. I'm sorry; truly sorry.' She paused. There was still one thing she needed to know before she committed herself to him. 'You and Rafe. You're very close.'

'Well — fairly, yes.'

'Because I have wondered if . . . if . . .'

'What?'

'Is Rafe your father?'

Lucas's astonishment was plain to see. 'Rafe, my father? Of course he isn't. Look.' He put a hand into his back trouser pocket and pulled out a leather wallet. From inside he extracted a photograph.

Christie found herself looking at what she could have been forgiven for thinking was a picture of Lucas.

'My father, taken just a year before he died.'

'Thank you.' She handed it back to him with a rueful smile. 'I've been wrong about everything, haven't I?'

He grinned back at her and murmured, 'Pretty well,' before his expression darkened and he said, 'Please don't leave. I can't lose you. I've never felt like this about any woman before. Tell me you feel the same. Because if you don't . . .'

'I do,' she blurted. 'I love you.'

'Oh, Christie, my darling.' His eyes glistened with emotion. 'If you knew how much I've longed to hear you say that. Ever since the first moment practically that I set eyes upon you. I couldn't believe what was happening to me.'

'Oh, Lucas, I felt the same way. I tried so hard to resist, but it was hopeless.'

'Thank goodness for that,' he drily retorted. 'Now I think we've wasted enough time, so come here.'

He held his arms out to her. Christie didn't hesitate; she walked straight into them. The kiss that followed drove everything else but him from her mind, and she knew in that moment that this was where she was meant to be; where she belonged — here with Lucas. She'd well and truly come home.

THE END

We do hope that you have enjoyed reading this large print book.

Did you know that all of our titles are available for purchase?

We publish a wide range of high quality large print books including:
**Romances, Mysteries, Classics
General Fiction
Non Fiction and Westerns**

Special interest titles available in large print are:
**The Little Oxford Dictionary
Music Book, Song Book
Hymn Book, Service Book**

Also available from us courtesy of Oxford University Press:
**Young Readers' Dictionary
(large print edition)
Young Readers' Thesaurus
(large print edition)**

For further information or a free brochure, please contact us at:
**Ulverscroft Large Print Books Ltd.,
The Green, Bradgate Road, Anstey,
Leicester, LE7 7FU, England.
Tel:** (00 44) **0116 236 4325
Fax:** (00 44) **0116 234 0205**

Other titles in the
Linford Romance Library:

HOLIDAY ROMANCE

Patricia Keyson

Dee, a travel rep, flies to the south of Spain to work at the Paradiso hotel. On the journey, a chance encounter with the half-Spanish model Freddie leads to the two spending time together, and she suspects she may be falling for him. Then Dee is introduced to Freddie's uncle, Miguel, who is particularly charming towards her — despite having only recently been in a relationship with fellow rep Karen. But when Karen disappears in suspicious circumstances, Dee must decide which man she can trust . . .